Bronson Howard

One of Our Girls

A Comedy in Four Acts

Bronson Howard

One of Our Girls
A Comedy in Four Acts

ISBN/EAN: 9783337054540

Printed in Europe, USA, Canada, Australia, Japan

Cover: Foto ©Andreas Hilbeck / pixelio.de

More available books at **www.hansebooks.com**

ONE OF OUR GIRLS

A Comedy in Four Acts

by

BRONSON HOWARD

CHARACTERS.

DR. GIRODET.

M. FONBLANQUE.

CAPT. JOHN GREGORY (Fifth Lancers).

COMTE FLORIAN DE CREBILLON.

HENRI SAINT-HILAIRE.

LE DUC DE FOUCHÉ-FONBLANQUE.

ANDRE.

PIERRE.

MME. FONBLANQUE.

JULIE.

MISS KATE SHIPLEY.

SOLICITOR.

SCENES.

PARIS.—The Chateau Fonblanque, and an Apartment in the Rue de Rivoli.

ACT I.

French Ideas and American Ideas.

An interval of six months.

ACT II.

An International Kiss.

ACT III.

IN TWO SCENES.

The French Result of a French Marriage.
An American Girl and an English Officer in a French Situation.

ACT IV.

A Scientific Experiment.

ONE OF OUR GIRLS.

ACT I.

SCENE.—*Apartment in the Chateau Fonblanque, in the suburbs of Paris. Richly furnished and upholstered. Large double doors up C. Doors up R., up L. and R. 1 E. Mantelpiece and fire down L. Large table, C., half up stage. Arm chairs, L. C. and R. Small table, R. High-backed chair up R. C. Small chairs, R. C. and up C. When the double doors at back are thrown open, a richly furnished drawing-room is seen.*

DISCOVERED.—M. FONBLANQUE, *sitting down,* L. C., *in thought.*

FONB. Our little daughter, Julie, is to sign her marriage contract this morning! It seems only yesterday that she was first brought to me in her nurse's arms.

[*Enter* DR. GIRODET, *up* R., *looking at a document in his hand.*]

You have finished with the solicitor, Francois?

DOCTOR. Yes. The marriage contract is quite correct, if it satisfies you. Thank heaven! I have had nothing to do with the document, except to save you the trouble of reading it over with the lawyers.

FONB. I am under great obligations to you, cousin. These business affairs always annoy me.

DOCTOR. And the marriage of a young girl is a strictly " business " affair. The solicitor says that the Count de Crebillon has insisted, to the last, that you told him Julie's dowry was to be six hundred and fifty thousand francs.

FONB. The Count assured me that the offer of his hand to my daughter was based on that amount.

DOCTOR. He threw in his heart for nothing. (*Aside.*) It's all it's worth!

FONB. I didn't care to insist on the difference between us; it was only fifty thousand francs.

DOCTOR. It would be a pity for a stern father to blast an ardent lover's affection for so small an amount. (*Gives* FONBLANQUE *the paper and turns away,* R.) I suppose it has become my duty, at last, Phillippe—my formal and painful duty—to congratulate you on Julie's approaching marriage.

FONB. Your "painful" duty! You have persisted in opposing this union from the first. The Count de Crebillon's title is one of the oldest and most honorable in France.

DOCTOR. His title? Yes. But the Count himself!

FONB. His ancestors——

DOCTOR.   His character!   When a family improves as it grows
older, it commands my most profound respect.   So does a cheese.
But in the case before us, if we test the cheese, I would say, the
family——

FONB.   The Crebillons of the fourteenth century figure most
conspicuously in the pages of Froissart's chronicles.

DOCTOR.   The Crebillons of the nineteenth century figure most
conspicuously in the columns of the sporting press.   The present
Count is a roué; a notorious duellist; and, without the dowry he
is about to gain with your daughter, he would soon add the honor-
ary degree of "Bankrupt" to that of "Gambler."   His first wife
was a disgrace to his title; but even she did less to dishonor it
than he, himself, has done.

FONB.   The Count has his peccadilloes, I admit.   As to his
first marriage, he appreciates the error very deeply; but, luckily,
there were no children.   The real question at issue is that of unit-
ing two streams of noble blood.   On all questions of that kind, my
dear Francois, your ideas are always—I may call them revolution-
ary; and, really, I object to them.

DOCTOR.   I dare say you object to the revolution of the earth
around the sun—because it wasn't mentioned in Froissart, and you
have grave doubts of the social respectability of the planetary
system.   The more recently discovered planets are mere parvenus.

FONB.   The Count de Crebillon's personal character is a mere
incident in the progress of a noble family.

DOCTOR.   And poor little Julie?   She, too, is a mere incident.

FONB.   Julie is delighted at the idea of becoming a married
woman.

DOCTOR.   I can quite understand that.   She longs to be free from
the restraints to which every young girl is condemned—in France,
at least—from infancy to matrimony.   She can see little or nothing of the world, and she dreams of pleasures in store for her
beyond her prison-bars.   Marriage, to a young French girl, means all
that freedom does to a convict.   Of course, Julie is happy at the
idea of becoming a married woman.   But does that fact relieve
you, cousin, of all responsibility for the character of the man
whom you have chosen for her husband?

FONB.   In marrying the Count, Julie merely fulfills her social
duty, in the position to which she was born.   Our own family
dates back many centuries——

DOCTOR.   Yes.   The original ape, from which the rest of the
human race descended, was a pet monkey in the Fonblanque family.   Phillippe, you are trying to unite two great French families
by a young girl's hand.   Mark my words—her heart will be
crushed between them!

[*Enter* MADAM FONBLANQUE, *up* R.]

MME. F.   I have just left our dear little Julie   She's the
brightest and merriest bride-elect that ever signed a marriage contract.   Her governess can do nothing with her; and her dressing-
maid can hardly keep her still long enough to arrange her hair.
(*Sitting*, R.)   Haven't you heard her laughing?

DOCTOR. (*Up* C.) I hope I shall hear her laugh in the future.

FONB. By-the-bye, my dear—(*Showing a note.*)—I received a letter from Henri Saint-Hilaire.

MME. F. (*Up* C.) From Henri!

FONB. He reached Paris, from South America, yesterday. I dare say he will be out here to-day.

MME. F. How very strange! Julie told me that she dreamed of Henri last night. I have been thinking of him, myself, continually of late.

DOCTOR. I have always hoped that Henri Saint-Hilaire would be something more to Julie than her old playfellow. For my own part, I heartily wish that he were in the place of the Count de Crebillon, to-day.

FONB. You are talking nonsense, Francois. I—I—love Henri, myself, very dearly.

MME. F. And I also; very dearly!

FONB. We always have—both of us. Henri was an excellent student, too; and he has already distinguished himself in his humble profession But he is a mere scientific man.

MME. F. We cannot forget our own blue blood, Francois.

FONB. Henri has no family whatever.

DOCTOR. No family! Etienne Geoffrey Saint-Hilaire! The discoverer of truths in science that have advanced the human race! Isidore Saint-Hilaire! Mere scientific men! Their names and their works have carried the glory of France beyond the reach of her armies. The Crebillons and the Fonblanques, mentioned by Froissart, were only preparing the way for such men as they! That is the family of Henri Saint-Hilaire!

[*Enter* PIERRE, *up* L.]

PIERRE. M. le Duc de Fouché-Fonblanque.

DOCTOR. Here's more Froissart. Damn Froissart!

[*Enter the* DUC DE FOUCHÉ-FONBLANQUE, *up* L. *Exit* PIERRE.]

DUC. Mathilde! Phillippe!

FONB. AND MME. F. Victorien!

DUC. Francois! (*To* DOCTOR, *bowing.*) My dear cousin.

DOCTOR. (*Bowing.*) On my mother's side.

DUC. I am quite aware that you are related to the Fonblanque family, on your mother's side, Doctor, but why do you mention the fact so particularly whenever *I* address you as my cousin?

DOCTOR. Out of respect for my father's memory.

DUC. Oh! That has something to do with science, I suppose. I never do know what you are talking about, Doctor. (*Turns down.*) I lost another hundred thousand at the races, yesterday, Phillippe. That makes nearly a million francs since January. I haven't been so lucky this year as I was last; I lost only *half* a million francs last year. Some one always tells me which horse is going to win, and I always bet on that horse; and then one of the other horses comes in first. Speaking of my losses, by-the-bye, some of my creditors are getting anxious. When did you say you expected Mme. Fonblanque's rich American niece from New York?

FONB. We may hear of her arrival at any moment, now.

DUC. I thought you said about this time. You wrote to her father, informing him that I would marry the girl as soon after her arrival in France as possible. Did you say anything about the dowry I should expect?

FONB. I asked him to communicate with me on that subject.

MME. F. We have received a photograph of Kate.

DUC. Oh! Her name is Kate.

MME. F. Here it is, Duc

DUC Thank you; I'll look at it, presently. What do you think we ought to put the dowry at, Cousin Phillippe? We must remember, of course, that Mr. Shipley is a—not exactly a common tradesman, I believe—but an ordinary business man; and only an American business man at that.

FONB. He is a banker and capitalist.

DOCTOR. (*Up* R. C) You mustn't sell your title too cheaply, Duc.

DUC. Pardon me, Doctor, but I don't like that word *sell*. A nobleman is *not* a common tradesman. As to this little American girl, herself, I must remember that she will come to me without education, or the manners of a lady. Of course, I know that she is your niece, Mathilde; but, as you sister ran away from France with an American husband, twenty years ago——

MME. F. Ah, Duc! it was a source of untold grief to us. Our families were never reconciled—until——

DOCTOR. Until Mr. Shipley had made a large fortune.

MME. F. Until we felt that further persistence in our family pride would be unchristian. When my sister returned to visit us, seven years ago, I wished to detain her daughter in France. If they had allowed me to do so, the girl would have been a refined and well-bred lady, now. As it is, you cannot expect the elegance of manner and the accomplishments, which have been beyond her reach, in a partially civilized country.

DUC. Of course not. I shall be obliged to introduce her to the ladies of my family; it will be a great trial to them.

MME. F. It will, indeed.

DUC I think the dowry should be at least twice as large as I should expect if I were conferring my hand and title on a lady of our own nationality.

MME. F. Quite double the amount.

[*Enter* PIERRE, *up* L.]

PIERRE. A letter, monsieur.

FONB. (*Taking it*) From New York. [*Exit* PIERRE, *up* L. This is Mr. Shipley's answer.

DUC. Ah! (*Sits*, C.)

FONB. (*Reading*.) "New York, March 21st, 1885. My dear Fonblanque: Kate will sail on the Ville de Paris to-morrow." This letter must have come by the same steamer; she is in France, now! (*Reads*.) "My bankers in Paris are Messrs. Drexel, Brown & Co. I have instructed them to accept Kate's checks to the amount of five thousand dollars. When she needs more, she will advise me by cable." Accept Kate's checks? A girl of nineteen doesn't know what the word " check " means!

MME. F. I'm sure Julie hasn't the slightest notion.

DOCTOR. I have been informed that American girls *do* understand the expression. An American patient of mine, in Paris, once told me that both his daughters used the word check frequently, in conversation with himself.

DUC. What does Mr. Shipley say about my approaching marriage with his daughter.

FONB. (*Reading*) " I remain, in haste, yours, etc., Robert G. Shipley."

DUC. Is that all there is in the letter?

FONB (*Reading.*) "Over." (*Turns page.*) A postscript!

DUC. A—a postscript!

FONB. (*Reading.*) " You spoke in one of your letters about some Duke that wants to marry my daughter."

DUC. Some—Duke?

FONB. "If his morals are good, I haven't any objection to him. He and Kitty may settle it between them. What business is the Duke in?"

(*The* DUC *starts to his feet. The* DOCTOR *shows suppressed laughter.*)

DUC. Business!—I!—in business!

DOCTOR. Send him your business card, Duke! (*Taking a card from table and continuing, as if reading from it.*) "Le Duc de Fonché-Fonblanque, speculator in thoroughbred horses—imported from England; and in wealthy young girls—imported from America."

DUC. " Kitty " and I—can " settle the matter "—between us? What has the girl, herself, to say about it? Mr. Shipley hasn't any objection to me!

DOCTOR. If your morals are good.

DUC. In the name of all that's incomprehensible, what have a gentleman's morals to do with his marrying another man's daughter?

DOCTOR. Nothing whatever—in France.

FONB. (*Rising*) Captain Gregory!

[*Enter* CAPTAIN JOHN GREGORY, *up* R.]

Good morning.

CAPTAIN. Good morning, M. Fonblanque! Madame! Duc! Dr. Girodet!

DUC. AND DOCTOR. Captain!

MME. F. I trust you have slept well—your first night at the Chateau Fonblanque.

CAPTAIN. Thank you, yes. Beautiful suburbs, Paris. I took a charming stroll this morning, about ten miles—all by myself. I'm enjoying my visit immensely.

[*Enter* PIERRE, *up* L., *with a card on silver.* FONBLANQUE *takes it.*]

FONB. Our niece, my dear! (*Reading.*) "Miss Kate Shipley, Park Avenue, New York." I will meet her.
[*Exit, up* L., *followed by* PIERRE.
DUC. The Indian Princess has arrived.
MME. F. A young American girl, Captain.
CAPTAIN. Ah! I never met any Americans, myself. (*Moving to mantel,* L.) Major Radclift, of our regiment, got acquainted with a number of Americans, once. *They* were girls. He told me they were rather nice. Most girls are rather nice!

(*Enter* KATE, *up* L., *followed by* FONBLANQUE. *She stops, up* L. C., *glancing about, quickly, then dropping her eyes. She looks up and advances a few steps towards* MME. FONBLANQUE, *who has risen.* KATE *stops, as if noticing her cool dignity of manner, and waits for her to speak.*)

MME. F. My niece!
KATE. Aunt!

(*She goes to her with a quick step, but stops, suddenly, before her, again checked by her manner.* MME. FONBLANQUE *kisses her forehead.*)

MME. F. We are glad to see you in France again, Kate.
KATE. I—I thank you. (*Choking*) Forgive me, madam, but—(*Touching her eyes.*)—when I first saw you, it—it seemed as if my own mother were standing before me. On the night she died, four years ago, she drew me to her breast, and kissed me; and she said that I must take that kiss—to her sister, in France.
MME. F. My child!

(*With some feeling, though still with calm dignity, taking* KATE'S *hand.* KATE *kisses her.*)

FONB. Let me introduce you to our friends, Kate. This is Dr. Girodet, a relative.
DOCTOR. You and I will be very good friends, my dear.
KATE. (*Heartily.*) I am *sure* we shall be, Doctor.
FONB. Captain Gregory, of the British Army; our niece.
CAPTAIN. Miss Shipley! (*Bowing.*)
KATE. (*Bowing.*) Captain!
CAPTAIN. (*Aside.*) *She's* rather nice!
FONB. Our cousin, the Duc de Fouché-Fonblanque. (*The* DUC *advances up* L. C., *bowing.*)
KATE. Duc! (*With a bow.*) I'm very glad to meet you, Captain Gregory.

(*Crossing to him, in front of* DUC. *The* DUC *rises from his bow, looking astonished, and turning to* DOCTOR.)

CAPTAIN. Thank you. I trust you had a pleasant voyage, Miss Shipley.
KATE. Charming!
FONB. It was a long distance for a young girl to come, alone, with no one but your governess in charge of you. (*Sitting,* R. C.)
KATE. My—governess—uncle? I'm nineteen years old.

MME. F. The same age as Julie.

KATE. Has Julie a governess?

MME. F. All young girls in France have, until they are married.

KATE. I am my own governess; and papa's, too. Every American girl is. Papa needed a governess badly, poor darling, after he lost dear mamma, until *I* was old enough to look after him. I keep house for him, aunt, and manage all the servants. If a girl doesn't learn how to govern herself before she's married, I don't see how she can govern her husband and the rest of her household afterwards. (*Sitting*, L. C.)

DUC. (*Aside*.) Govern—her—husband!

KATE. I arrived in Paris on Tuesday evening, and should have come out here at once, only I had so many purchases to make. I bought two new trunks, and I filled them both. I wanted to see my bankers, too.

DUC. (*Aside*.) Her bankers!

MME. F. (*Aside*.) A young girl of nineteen with a banker!

KATE. Papa gave me some New York Central shares for my last birthday present, and, just before I sailed, he wanted to sell them for me. But they were only ninety-nine cents, and the Secretary of the company is Superintendent of our Sunday School. The clergyman told me that he whispered to him, on the previous Sunday, while he was changing his gown in the vestry, just before the sermon, that New York Central shares were sure to go up. So I told papa not to sell mine. My bankers in Paris told me, yesterday, that they were a hundred and ten! Dear papa! I never could get him to go to church, but he'll go regularly after this!

FONB. You say you have no governess; but surely you were not alone on the voyage.

KATE. Oh, no! A family—old friends of ours—came on the same steamer; a father and mother and their two sons. I was never alone; one of the young gentlemen was always with me.

MME. F. (*Aside*.) One of the gentlemen!

KATE. The party came as far as Rouen, also, on the train from Havre. I came the rest of the way alone.

FONB. All the way from Rouen to Paris! It was very unsafe, my dear girl!

MME. F. And highly imprudent!

KATE. I have traveled hundreds of miles alone, in America; why not here? But I confess my first experience was an extremely disagreeable one. A gentleman sat opposite to me, when we left Rouen. That is, I mistook him for a gentleman at first, because I heard his servant address him as a "Count" before the train started.

DUC. You were alone in the compartment with a—a Count!

KATE. All alone, Duc!—with a French Count—in a French train—on a French railway—in France. To tell the truth, the Count made himself exceedingly disagreeable to me the first five miles.

DOCTOR. My child!

MME. F. What did you do?

KATE. I looked him straight in the eye, for the *next* five miles; and he changed his compartment at the first station.

CAPTAIN. (*Aside.*) If I were charging a redoubt, I shouldn't like to meet an American girl on top of it.

FONB. You must never expose yourself to such a risk again, Kate.

KATE. I never shall. If I ever again see a nobleman in a railway train, I'll get into another compartment. But Cousin Julie! I'm longing to see her again.

FONB. You have come just in time to witness the signing of her marriage contract.

KATE. What's that, uncle?

FONB. Have they no such ceremony in America!

KATE. The only marriage contract I ever heard of is where a gentleman asks a young lady to be his wife, and she says "no" and changes it to "yes" before he has time to drop her hand; then they kiss each other. That's the American ceremony. But we never have any witnesses to the contract!

MME. F. Allow me to remark, my niece, that a gentleman in France is never permitted to be alone with a young lady, even after they are engaged to be married, much less to kiss her!

KATE. It's different in America. I've never been engaged myself, but a lot of other girls I know have been. When two young people, there, are making love, other people get to the furthest room in the house, and shut all the doors between. If anyone looks into the parlor, he dodges back as if he'd just thought of an engagement somewhere else. Two lovers in America are put in quarantine. They might as well be on a desert island together—but they never seem to be lonely!

MME. F. Do gentlemen in your country make love to young ladies in person, then?

KATE. They'd all die old bachelors if they didn't. You are in the Fifth Lancers, Captain Gregory?

CAPTAIN. Yes.

KATE. I met Major Radclift, of your regiment, in Paris, yesterday.

CAPTAIN. Oh!

KATE. He said you were visiting here.

CAPTAIN. Ah!

KATE. He told me you were the bravest officer in the regiment.

CAPTAIN. Yes. I mean—exactly—that is—of course—I would say—I—I beg your pardon—(*Moving up.*)—but I haven't had my regular exercise this morning; I'll take a few turns in the garden. (*Aside.*) Damn Major Radclift!   [*Exit, up L.*

DOCTOR. Captain Gregory never beat a retreat like that in the face of an enemy.

[*Enter* PIERRE, *up L.*]

PIERRE. M. le Comte de Crebillon has arrived, M. Fonblanque.

FONB. (*Rising. To* DUC.) Will you join us, Duc?

DUC. With pleasure. [*Exit* FONBLANQUE, *up L., followed by* PIERRE.] Au revoir, Miss Kate!

KATE. Au revoir! By-the-bye, Duc, my father received a letter from uncle just before I left New York.

DUC. Yes?

KATE. About a matter of business.

DUC (*Aside*) Business! (*Aloud.*) I requested M. Fonblanque to address your father

KATE. I am papa's agent. But I'll not detain you, now. We will settle the - business—at some future time.

DUC. Yes. (*Aside, going.*) I've proposed to an American girl! I'll leave it to my lawyer. I could never manage it myself.

[*Exit, up L.*

DOCTOR. (*Aside, sitting at table, up* C.) I suspect the Duc's creditors will have to wait awhile for that dowry. (MME. FON-BLANQUE *rises*, R. KATE *rises*, L.)

MME. F. The apartments prepared for you, Kate, are at your service.

KATE. Thank you, aunt; but I left all my trunks at the hotel, to follow me.

MME. F. (*Aside.*) All her trunks!

DOCTOR. (*Aside.*) Opening skirmish of the campaign—a French aunt and an American niece. (*A book or paper before him.*)

MME. F. Did I understand you to say that you were alone in the streets of Paris, yesterday and the day before?

KATE. Yes, aunt.

MME. F. Surely, there was a maid, at least, with you.

KATE. I never had a maid. It's bad enough to look after the other servants.

MME. F. Permit me to say that no young lady, in Paris, is expected to be seen on the streets without a suitable companion.

KATE. If a girl can't be trusted alone at nineteen, aunt, she can't be at ninety. I spent all yesterday afternoon at the Louvre gallery.

MME. F. The Louvre! No young girl should visit a public gallery without a governess, or other older companion. They all contain many pictures which are highly improper for a young girl.

KATE. I hadn't any governess to point out the improper pictures, so I looked at the others. My friends came on from Rouen, and joined me again, yesterday noon. One of the young gentlemen took me to a concert in the evening.

MME. F. I am positively shocked! You—you went out—in the evening—with a gentleman!

KATE. Yes, aunt.

MME. F. Let me say to you, once for all, that nothing whatever of that kind must ever occur again, while you are under my roof.

KATE. Surely, aunt, when a young lady is entrusted to a gentleman's care, he is her natural protector until she returns to her home.

MME. F. I dare say you have invented a new kind of young man in America.

KATE. There must be *some* gentlemen, here, that can be trusted like that. What kind of young men do girls *marry* in France—nice girls, I mean—like Julie and me?

MME. F. I will converse with you further, my niece, when we are at leisure, on the customs to which young girls are expected to conform in countries more civilized than America.

KATE. Thank you, aunt. I will try to do everything I can to please you, while I am a visitor at your house. If I find it impossible to do so, without sacrificing my own self-respect, I shall cease, of course, to be a visitor.

(*They both bow with great dignity.* MME. FONBLANQUE *moves up L.*)

DOCTOR. (*Aside.*) End of the first encounter. There'll be plenty more! (*Rising.*)

MME. F. You will assist M. Fonblanque and myself in receiving our guests, Francois?

DOCTOR. I will follow you, madame.

[*Exit* MME. FONBLANQUE, *up* L.

[JULIE *runs in, gaily, up* R.]

JULIE. Uncle Francois! (*Throws her arms around the neck of the* DOCTOR, *who receives her in his arms.*) I'm going to be a married woman, uncle! Just think of it! (*Laughing.*) A married woman!

DOCTOR. My pet! I hope you will always come to me with a smile like that on your face.

(*Kisses her and turns to go. He turns again, throws her a kiss, smiling, and goes out, up* L. JULIE *throws a kiss after him, then turns down* C. *She stops, abruptly, and looks at* KATE.)

JULIE. Why! It isn't—Oh!

KATE. (*Extending her arms.*) Julie!

JULIE. Kate! (*The two girls are clasped in each other's arms.*) I've been wishing so much you could be here, to-day. Let me look at you! Take off your hat! (*Taking her hat.*) There! (*Drawing back and looking at her.*) I'd have known you anywhere; and yet—you have changed, too; you—you seem like a woman, now.

KATE. And you seem to me the same sweet, innocent girl of twelve that I remember you—seven years ago.

JULIE. Yes; and I am very tired of being a sweet, innocent girl. Aren't you? But I am to be married, in a few weeks, and —oh! I can be your chaperon!

KATE. (*Laughing.*) My chaperon!

JULIE. You won't be obliged to have your governess with you all the time. Have you a nice governess? I have. She never tells mamma anything I do. Ha, ha, ha! I ran away from governess, in Paris, last week, and I was all alone on the streets for nearly two hours! I was almost run over, once; but it was such fun! Ha, ha, ha! I went into the Champs Élysées all by myself!

Governess found me, at last, in front of one of the marionette shows; she was awfully frightened, but she never said a word about it to mamma. If your governess isn't a nice one, you shall have mine, as soon as I m married.

KATE. Thank you, my dear; I'm perfectly satisfied with my own governess; when I do anything wrong, she never calls any-one's attention to it. But now you must tell me, darling—(*Putting her arm around her waist, and walking to and fro.*)—all about your marriage. You must be very happy.

JULIE. Yes; I am. My trousseau will be lovely!

KATE. Is the gentleman light or dark?

JULIE. He has dark hair and eyes, I believe, but I barely noticed him when he called.

(KATE *stops, l. c., drops her arms from* JULIE's *waist, and falls back, step by step, staring at her.*)

Mamma didn't tell me, till just before he came, that he was to be my husband; and it seemed so strange, you know. I hardly raised my eyes; and the room was rather dark, too. My wedding dress is to be white brocaded satin, with a long train—it will be the first train I ever had—with sprays of orange blossoms run-ning——

KATE. You are going to marry a man you have never seen but once—and you didn't look at him, then—and the room was dark!

JULIE. The Count was obliged to leave Paris that afternoon.

KATE. Oh! He's a Count.

JULIE. Yes. A gentleman usually calls at least twice before the contract is signed, but he wrote to father and apologized. He couldn't get back until this morning.

KATE. Didn't he ever propose to *you?*

JULIE. The Count proposed to father for my hand, of course.

KATE. Why didn't you tell him to *marry* your father?

JULIE. Ha, ha, ha, ha! It's quite immaterial to me which of us he marries.

KATE. You do not love him, Julie! You cannot, of course.

JULIE. Love him? No; I'm only going to marry him!

KATE. Oh! That's all!

JULIE. Married! I can go where I please, and see what I please. I can meet anyone I like—and there must be a lot of nice, wicked things in the world that an innocent young girl doesn't know anything about. I'm to be a married woman!

KATE. Ah! I see. A canary to be suddenly released from its cage! We American birds are bred in the open air, Julie; we're a little wild, perhaps, but we choose our own mates; and we settle down very comfortably in our nests, with them, afterwards. Do girls really marry men, in France, before they have listened to words of tenderness and affection from their lips? It doesn't seem—forgive me, Julie—but it doesn't seem modest and womanly to me for a girl to become a man's wife before she has heard such words—before they have even kissed each other.

JULIE. Kissed each other! Oh! That would be very wrong—before marriage.

KATE. If a girl doesn't love a man so much she can't help kissing him, she oughtn't to marry him at all. But you and I can't make each other understand these things. We have been brought up so far apart, and in such different countries. We'll talk about old times, when we were children together; we understood each other perfectly, then. Is the old garden just as it used to be? And—oh!—where is the big boy, now, that used to play with us? He was three or four years older than we were; the one that was visiting here.

JULIE. Henri Saint-Hilaire?

KATE. Yes; that was his name.

JULIE. Henri went away from France soon afterwards; but he came back for a few months about two years ago, and he visited here, again. Do you remember the old well, Kate, down in the furthest and darkest corner of the garden?

KATE. Yes, indeed, I do, and the story about it. If a girl sees a gentleman's face beside her own, when she looks down into the water, on a moonlight night—that gentleman will be her husband. We girls used to climb up and look over the curb, but, ha, ha, ha, ha! we always omitted a very important part of the ceremony; we didn't take the gentleman with us.

JULIE. I did see a face beside mine, one evening, about two years ago. It was during Henri's last visit; the very night before he went away again. Ha, ha, ha! It was such a lark! I ran around one side of the château, and Henri ran around the other side. Governess saw us coming back, but she never said anything about it.

KATE. The story of the old well won't turn out true in this case, Julie!

JULIE. (*With a shade of momentary sadness.*) Of course not. It *couldn't* turn out true. Henri doesn't belong to an old French family, as I do (*Then brightening and looking around, laughingly, her fingers to her lips.*) H—s—h! I'll tell you a secret. Henri kissed me at the old well! Ha, ha, ha!

KATE. You said, just now, that it was wrong, in France, to allow a gentleman to kiss you, before you are married to him.

JULIE. But I'm not going to marry Henri.

KATE. Oh!

JULIE. Besides, there was nobody looking, and *that* isn't wrong, in any country! Ha, ha, ha, ha! Henri gave me his picture, set around with diamonds, which he had gathered for me, himself, in Brazil. Here it is; you shall see how he looked two years ago. (*Takes miniature from her dress, suspended by a ribbon to her neck.*)

KATE. You are wearing that picture, on your breast—to-day? To-day, Julie?

JULIE. I've worn it there ever since Henri gave it to me. I shall tell him so when he comes back to Paris. He'll be very glad to learn I've always remembered him. What fun we used to have together. Ha, ha, ha! (*Laughing and kissing the picture.*) This looks exactly as he did then.

KATE. I hope Henri Saint-Hilaire will never return to Paris.

JULIE. Oh, yes; he's on his way home, now.

KATE. Julie! (*Earnestly, laying her hand on her arm.*) You must never see him.

JULIE. Why! Ha, ha, ha, ha! What queer notions you American girls do have about everything! (*Moving* R., *up stage.*) When I'm a married woman, Henri and I can see each other as often as we like.

KATE. Julie! Julie!

[*Enter* FONBLANQUE, *up* L.]

FONB. Ah, Julie, you are here.

(*Enter the* COUNT DE CREBILLON, *up* L. KATE *moves down* R. FONBLANQUE *crosses to* JULIE, *up stage*, L. *The* COUNT *moves down* L. *He and* KATE *see each other. She starts and looks him, firmly, in the eye. He looks at her, steadily, a moment, then turns away.*)

COUNT. (*Aside.*) The little American Gorgon that stared me out of countenance, the other day!

FONB. Julie, my darling, your mother and I must soon give you up—to one who will care for your happiness hereafter, as we have done till now. Count! (*Leading* JULIE *across.*) We are giving you, to-day, the treasure of our house and of our hearts.

KATE. Her husband!

COUNT. I trust that I shall be worthy of such a gift.

(*Taking* JULIE'S *hand, leaning over it, gracefully, and kissing it.* JULIE *stands before him, with down-cast eyes.*)

KATE. Uncle!

FONB. Kate! Pardon me! The Count de Crebillon! Our niece!

KATE. I wish to speak with you, uncle, on a subject which concerns Julie's happiness—for life.

FONB. Your mother has gone to your room, Julie. The Count and I will join you both in the drawing-room.

(JULIE *moves up, across* R. *Looks back.*)

JULIE. My happiness—for life! Everybody has something to do with that, except myself.   [*Exit, up* R.

KATE. Alone, if you please, Count!

(*The* COUNT *inclines his head and passes up* L. *He turns and bows, deeply, to* KATE, *who now bows low, in return. Exit* COUNT, *up* L.)

My dear uncle, I told you that a stranger, on the way from Rouen, made himself offensive to me, by his attention. I did not tell you all. I could not, then. The man insulted me! He was the Count de Crebillon!

FONB. Indeed! A most unfortunate coincidence. The Count will be glad, of course, to apologize, both to you and me, for the mistake he made.

KATE. Apologize—for—his—mistake!

FONB. I trust it will be a lesson to you. The mistake was a natural one. A respectable young girl, in France, is not expected to place herself in such a compromising position. You must be more careful in future. As to the Count, himself, believe me, he will treat you, hereafter, with the most profound respect.

[*Exit, up* L.

KATE. A lesson—to *me!* Such a man as that is considered a proper husband for a young girl—and Julie will sign her marriage contract with the picture of another in her bosom! This is France! My mother's country! But you left it, mother, with the husband your own heart had chosen. Julie! My poor Julie! What must be the end ?

[*Enter* PIERRE, *followed by* HENRI SAINT-HILAIRE, *up* L.]

HENRI. I'll not go into the drawing-room, Pierre. I'll wait here till they are at liberty. (*Coming down* L. C. *Exit* PIERRE, *up* R. HENRI *sees* KATE.) I beg your pardon.

KATE. M. Henri Saint-Hilaire! I recognized you at once.

HENRI. Is it not the little American girl, that——

KATE. Yes, monsieur. I am the same little American girl— (*Extending her hand, frankly.*)—that you knew at Chateau Fonblanque, seven years ago.

HENRI. (*Taking her hand.*) I'm very glad to see you here again. I often think of you, when I am thinking of Julie. I have not seen *her* for two years. She is in the drawing-room with the others, I suppose.

KATE. (*Looking down.*) Yes! She is there, with the rest. (*Then raising her head, looking straight into his eyes, speaking slowly and distinctly.*) Our little playmate is going to sign her marriage contract, this morning.

HENRI. Ah! (*With a gasp, starting back.*) Her marriage contract!

KATE. Oh! I feared it *might* be a blow to you, Henri; but you ought to know the truth at once.

HENRI. Julie!—to be married to another! It is for this that I have struggled—for this that I have been dreaming of her, in a foreign land—for an end like this. Another's wife! Julie! Julie!

(*Enter* PIERRE, *up* R., *with large inkstand and pens. He is followed by an elderly gentleman, the* SOLICITOR, *with the contract in his hand.* PIERRE *places the inkstand, etc., on the table. The* SOLICITOR *lays the contract on table and opens it.*)

SOLICITOR. (*To* PIERRE.) The contract is quite ready.

(PIERRE *throws open the double doors at back. Guests are seen : Ladies and gentlemen in groups. Among them are the* CAPTAIN, *the* DUC *and* DR. GIRODET; *also* M. *and* MME. FONBLANQUE, JULIE *and the* COUNT. *The* SOLICITOR *offers the pen, bowing to the* COUNT, *who moves down. A general movement down through the double doors, the guests forming a background of the picture. The* COUNT *takes the pen, turns and bows to* JULIE; *then signs the contract. He then extends the pen to* JULIE, *who moves down and takes it. She sees* HENRI.)

JULIE. Oh! Henri! (*She drops the pen and runs down, laughing, brightly, and extending her hands.*) You've come back already. (*Henry takes her hand, eagerly.*) I'm very, very glad to see you again.

HENRI. Julie!

COUNT. Shall we finish the signing of the marriage contract, mademoiselle? (*With the pen in his hand.*)

JULIE. Eh? Oh, yes, of course! I forgot! Ha, ha, ha, ha!

(*She runs across, takes the pen and is signing the contract as the curtain descends.* HENRI *is looking steadily at* JULIE. *The* COUNT *is looking at* HENRI; KATE *from* JULIE *to* HENRI.)

CURTAIN.

ACT II.

AN INTERVAL OF SIX MONTHS BETWEEN ACT I. AND ACT II.

SCENE.—*The Chateau Fonblanque. Another apartment, opening upon garden. Perforated windows at back, similar doors up L., and window down L., all looking to garden, in which ornamental lanterns hang among the trees. The right upper corner of the apartment opens by arches to large room beyond. Door, R. 1. Upright piano down L. Chair and small table, L. C. Ottomans, R. C. and L. C. Small escritoire, R. of C., with chair A lamp, lighted, on escritoire is the only light of this apartment. Moonlight over the garden and streaming through the window and door, L., while the effect of a dim light in the room is to be secured by the painting, the lamp, etc. The actual light on the stage should be almost full; apartment beyond brilliantly lighted.*

DISCOVERED.—KATE, *sitting at escritoire. She is arranging paper, etc., as the curtain rises.*

KATE. (*Writing.*) "My own darling papa: I've just spent three mortal hours at the dinner table, and there's a grand reception to follow, at eleven. The gentlemen are still at their cigars. I have run away from the ladies to write you a letter in time for to-morrow's mail. I was trying on all my lovely new dresses this afternoon, so I hadn't time to write before. There were sixteen people at dinner—m - m—m—(*Continuing, as if giving words or lines as she writes.*)—m—m. Awfully full dress. Ambassadors in court costumes, officials in all their decorations, and military officers in their full uniforms—m—m—m—m. The young English officer I told you about—the one that was visiting here when I first came —he has come back from England again, and is now living in Paris. He is here to-night, and he sat next to me at dinner." (*Speaks.*) He told me that he couldn't stay away from France. It's very curious—I didn't tell him so—but, after he returned to London, I found it all I could do to keep away from England. (*Writes.*) "I am dressed in pistache ottoman silk and velvet to match, and"—(*Speaks.*)—Father won't understand a word of that. (*Writes.*) "It cost seven hundred dollars." (*Speaks.*) He'll understand that. I know they're all awfully shocked at my costume to-night, especially by the diamonds. A young girl in France isn't allowed to wear diamonds at all; but give any American girl a pair of solitaire earrings, and look at her ears the next time you meet her—no matter where. They regard me here as a wild, young Indian Princess, anyway. I might as well dress like one and enjoy myself. They ought to be glad I have anything

on, except a string of beads around my waist. For the last five
months, since Julie was married to the Count, and I've been the
only unmarried girl in the house, aunt has been holding her
breath all the time to see what I'd do next; an American girl, in
Paris, is always doing something next, and its always the very
last thing the people here expect a girl to do. They think a
young woman ought to be so fresh and "innocent," as they call
it. Well! I tried as hard as I could to please aunt, at first. I
haven't any objection to being innocent for a few months, but,
somehow, I can't understand French innocence; and they can't
understand my sort of innocence. So now I'm just my own
American self; and that's all I intend to be. I'll surprise 'em
with a war whoop one of these days. (*Writes.*) "Papa, dear,
they can't make me out, here, at all. I'm shocking everybody
awfully, and I'm getting worse and worse every day. Poor, dear
aunt reminds me of a very dignified elderly hen with one chicken
to look after, and that chicken a duck. My languages come in
very nicely with the foreign swells here. I've been talking
German with a Grand Duke, to-night, and Italian to a Prince; but,
whatever language I talk in, I seem to shock people, all the
same." (*Speaks.*) I verily believe they're astonished to hear me
talk any human language. I'll learn Choctaw before I come
again, and confine myself to it; that's the only way an American
girl can keep from shocking people in Europe. As to my other
accomplishments—Ha, ha, ha!—when I played one of Beethoven's
sonatas in B flat, the other day, that fat Marchioness nearly
choked with astonishment; and I ended it off so suddenly with
"Yankee Doodle" that she nearly tipped over backwards on the
little Spanish Count. If she had, there'd 'a been one less foreign
ambassador at dinner to-day. Ha, ha, ha! For the life of me, I
couldn't help telling him, when he complimented me on my playing
a classical selection, that I picked it all up in Europe during the
last six months, and that New York ladies never played on anything at home but a tom-tom; and they went about bare-footed,
except on Sunday, and then they went to church in moccasins,
embroidered with beads. (*Writes.*) "The worst of it is, papa,
they believe everything one says about America, and I can't help
telling them awful fibs. I'd die if I didn't." (*Speaks.*) I believe
that nice, old, French Field-Marshal half suspected I wasn't telling him the exact truth, to-night, when he got his wig twisted
over his left ear, and I tried to make it pleasant for him by saying
that nearly all American gentlemen over thirty years old wore
wigs, because they usually scalped each other before that age.
I've often heard father talk about his best friend being scalped,
right in Wall Street. It would have been all right if I'd stopped
there, for it didn't surprise him a bit; it seemed to be exactly
what he expected Americans to do to each other. To save my
life, I couldn't help going on till I thought of something that
would surprise him. When I told him that an American kept his
eye on the top of his enemy's head every time he met him with
his hat off, and as soon as his hair began to grow thin he scalped
him at once before it was too late, the old gentleman did have a

puzzled expression, then. (*Writes.*) "If anyone ever tells them the truth about some things I've told 'em here, there'll be war between France and America." Ha, ha, ha, ha, ha! (*Leaning back and laughing very heartily. Speaks.*) If I were in the drawing-room, now, with aunt and the other French ladies all looking on me as a young female barbarian, I—I'd be dancing a war-dance among 'em! I know I should! Ha, ha, ha, ha! (*Springing to her feet and dancing in a dainty, half imitation of an Indian war-dance, laughing, gaily, as she does it, and giving herself up to the spirit of mischief.*) Ha, ha, ha, ha! I can imagine the fat Marchioness staring at me through her glasses, and poor, dear aunt, resigned to her fate, as a dowager duchess at her elbow remarks: "A native American custom, I suppose." Ha, ha, ha, ha!

(*Enter* CAPTAIN GREGORY, *from apartment up* R., *in full Lancer's uniform, evening dress. He stops and looks at her through his single glass. She sees him and stops dancing, suddenly.*)

Oh! Ha, ha, ha, ha! You shall dance, too, Captain. (*Runs across to piano and plays* "Yankee Doodle," *with great spirit and full, rattling accompaniment; stops suddenly and looks over her shoulder.*) You're not dancing. Perhaps you prefer a different air. (*Plays* "God Save the Queen," *singing the last few words of the stanza.*) Is that more to your fancy?

CAPTAIN. I think those two airs go particularly well together. I hope they always will go together, and I never wished so so much, as—as since I found myself a visitor at the same house, six months ago, with an American girl, Miss Kate, in a foreign country.

KATE. When you left us, Captain, it seemed as though I was further from my own country than ever; and when you came back to live in Paris, the Atlantic Ocean didn't seem half as wide. The only time I ever feel quite at home here is when I see your English face, and when I hear you speak our language, even if you don't speak it exactly as I do.

CAPTAIN. I learned French in Paris, but I never had a chance to acquire the correct English accent in New York.

KATE. (*Rising and crossing,* R.) I shall be delighted to teach you how to speak your own language, Captain. (*Aside.*) And I'll teach him what to say to me in it, too, if I can.

CAPTAIN. (*Crossing,* L.) I could take lessons from a dear little nose like her's all day.

KATE. Do I ever shock you, Captain, as I do the rest of them here.

CAPTAIN. Frequently. (*She turns, abruptly, drawing up.*) I like to be shocked.

KATE. Oh!

CAPTAIN. Shock me again! It's delightful!

KATE. I'm just finishing a letter to father. (*Sitting at escritoire,* R. C.)

CAPTAIN. I'll stroll into the garden.

KATE. Don't go, please. I'll be ready to shock you again in a moment. I've only to send my love, and sign my name, and put in the postscript.

CAPTAIN. (*Aside.*) Her love!

KATE. (*Writing.*) "He has just come in, and he looks so nice in his uniform." (*Looks over her shoulder at him.*)

CAPTAIN. (*Aside.*) I've been trying to tell that girl I love her for the last three weeks, only they never gave me a chance to be alone with her; and now I *am* alone with her I don't know how to begin.

KATE. (*Writing.*) "I love him more and more." Oh! stupid!

CAPTAIN. Eh?

KATE. (*Altering a word.*) "I love you more and more—(*Writing.*)—dear papa."

CAPTAIN. She was thinking of some other fellow. Whoever he is, he can't be stupider than I am. How do fellows talk to girls when they're really in love with them?

KATE. (*Writing*) "A dozen warm kisses." (*Kisses her hand to him, behind his back.*)

CAPTAIN. Miss Kate! (*Turning; she turns back, just in time to avoid being caught.*)

KATE. (*Writing.*) "For you, papa."

CAPTAIN. I beg your pardon.

KATE. "Your loving daughter, Kate." (*Folds letter, etc.*) You were about to say, Captain—— (*Rising.*)

CAPTAIN. I was—I was merely going to—to—from the very first moment I saw you, Miss Kate——

KATE. One moment, please. (*Returns to escritoire; opens letter and writes.*) "Postscript. I feel that something very serious is going to happen to-night, papa." Go on, Captain.

CAPTAIN. When I returned to London, I found I couldn't—I—well—I came back to Paris and took apartments, so that I could be near to—to—and—then I—then I met you again, you know. (*Aside.*) I wonder what father said to mother when he proposed.

KATE. (*Writing.*) "I shall have something very important to tell you in my next letter!"

CAPTAIN. (*Aside.*) If a fellow could overhear his father, he'd know the right thing to say, himself, when his own turn came, because a fellow's father succeeded—of course!

KATE. Did you ever see the old well, Captain, down at the foot of the garden, hidden away among bushes and creepers, where only the moonlight can reach it?

CAPTAIN. I stumbled on it one morning when I was visiting here. Queer old place.

KATE. I think I'll stroll down to it now. (*Crossing, L.; stops at door, in the moonlight. Aside.*) I wonder if I shall see his face there, beside mine. (*Aloud.*) I'm not a bit afraid of going alone, Captain. You—you needn't follow me.

(*Exit into garden, L. The* CAPTAIN *looks after her a moment, then moves up to door.*)

CAPTAIN. It looks awfully dark out there, beyond the lights, for a girl, alone——

[*Enter* JULIE, *from apartment, up* R.]

JULIE. Strolling into the garden, Captain?
CAPTAIN. I was going to light another cigar. (*Exit to garden.*)
JULIE. (*Looking out after him.*) Kate is there, too! She has disappeared beyond the rose bush. They are going to the well, together—as—as—Heigh-ho!—as Henri Saint-Hilaire and I did, once. It is years—it seems so many years!—since that night. (*Coming down; takes the miniature from her breast.*) How little I knew that Henri's face, looking up at me from the water, was engraved so deeply in my heart. I was only a careless young girl, then. I hardly knew I had a heart. Kate can choose for herself. (*At casement, down L., looking out, the moonlight falling on her.*) She will carry her husband's picture in her breast. We women in France are not allowed to do that. Ah! (*She gives a short, quick scream, springing back a few steps.*) A face staring at me—a woman's face!

(*She moves, cautiously, towards the window again, peering out.* HENRI SAINT-HILAIRE *enters*, R. *front, from apartment. He stops*, R., *looking at her.*)

It is gone. She was not one of the servants. (*Turning.*) Henri!
HENRI. I have been looking for you—to say good-bye.
JULIE. You are going early.
HENRI. I leave France to-morrow.
JULIE. What do you mean Henri?
HENRI. I shall return to South America, to continue the studies in which I was engaged before I hurried home, a few months ago.
JULIE. This is a sudden resolution.
HENRI. No; I made the resolution long ago—but I—Heigh-ho! I have not acted upon it.
JULIE. Will you—be gone—long—Henri?
HENRI. If I ever return——
JULIE. Ever!
HENRI. It will be many years from now. I shall always think of you as one of my dearest friends, as the little playmate of my boyhood, and it will be pleasant to feel that you are thinking of me in the same way.
JULIE. You—you are going away—perhaps—forever!
HENRI. Yes. I must go. Good-bye.

(*Extends his hand. She extends hers, but withdraws it as it touches his, turning away.*)

JULIE. To-morrow! And you will leave me alone! Alone?
HENRI. I leave you with your friends; with your parents and —— (*Hesitates.*)
JULIE. And—my—husband. I am never so utterly alone as when I am with *him*.
HENRI. Julie!

JULIE. Terribly alone! I must lead the life of solitude now to which I have been condemned by my marriage. I was ignorant of the world—almost ignorant of right and wrong—they call it "innocence"—and I was given to him! I did not think of love. He did not expect it from me, nor care for it. I was perfectly contented with that, at first, but I am bound to a man who would despise a woman's heart if she could give it to him; a man so cold, and cynical, and heartless, that I shrink from him almost with terror, whenever he is in my presence. (*Sinking upon ottoman,* L. C.) A woman cannot live and not love, Henri. You have been near me, too. (*Hides face in hands.*)

HENRI. We—we ought not to have been near each other.

JULIE. Do not despise me, Henri! Do not despise me!

HENRI. I am despising myself for having been here, to profit by your misery. He is your husband, Julie, and I have no place between you. When I came back to France and found you promised to another, there was but one manly and honorable course before me. I was a coward, and I did not take that course. I should have returned at once to my work, but I remained in Paris. I have allowed myself to be a constant visitor here, as in the old times, when we were children. I—I—have determined to be a coward no longer. I shall leave France to-morrow. Good-bye. (*Extending his hand.*)

JULIE. Good-bye.

(*Slowly reaching out her hand, back of her, without turning. He takes it, presses it to his own, drops it by her side and moves back, still looking at her.*

Alone with him!

HENRI. I am, indeed, leaving her alone. She shrinks from her husband in terror, now! What has the future in store for her? I shall only live on and suffer, for the memory of my love. But she, tender, and gentle, and weak, is bound to one who will crush her young life out—slowly but surely! Julie! (*Impulsively moving towards her.*) I pity you, with my whole heart! (*Dropping to his knees at the side of the ottoman, and seizing her hand.*) I pity you, my poor girl, I pity you.

JULIE. Henri.

(*He is pressing her hand to his lips. Enter the* COUNT, *from apartment, up* R., *with cigar. He stops, up* R. C., *and looks at them.*)

HENRI. I shall suffer, too, Julie; I shall suffer, too. Fate has been cruel to us both.

COUNT. M. Saint-Hilaire!

(HENRI *starts to his feet, stepping back,* L., *and facing the* COUNT. JULIE *rises and moves to* R. C.)

HENRI. Count de Crebillon!

COUNT. (*To* JULIE, *at her side.*) Go into the drawing-room at once, and join the other ladies. (*She retires, step by step,* R., *under fear and emotion.*)

JULIE. They will meet! Henri will be killed! (*Then, with a sudden thought.*) Uncle Francois! I will speak to him. He will prevent it.   [*Exit, R., by apartment.*

HENRI. Count! Believe me, your wife is spotless. I had just bade her farewell, intending to leave France to-morrow, forever. My own feelings overcame me at the last moment. She is not responsible for those feelings. I need hardly add, however, that I am responsible.

COUNT. You have arranged to leave France, to-morrow? We will settle the matter before morning, if you like.

HENRI. The sooner the better.

COUNT. We need not disturb the company. We can arrange the affair quietly between ourselves during the evening. Au revoir, monsieur.

HENRI. Au revoir, Count.

(*The* COUNT *strikes a match and is re-lighting his cigar as he goes out to garden, up* L. *Enter the* DOCTOR, *up* R., *from apartment. He watches the* COUNT *going, then turns to Henri.*)

DOCTOR. Henri! Was it for this that I watched over you in childhood and youth, as if I were your father? I saw, with tender interest, your growth in knowledge; I have seen you adding new honor to the name which your grandfather made illustrious in science. Have you learned nothing better from kindly nature than to crush a beautiful flower—like Julie?

HENRI. Oh! Doctor Girodet. I should not have been here to-night. I should have fled from temptation many months ago. I have tried to do so over and over again, but the struggle was too great for me. Oh! If you only knew how I have struggled. I have loved Julie from my boyhood, when she was a little thing that came to my arms as innocently as a bird might rest in my hand. When I saw her again, after a long absence, a girl of seventeen, it was with a man's heart, and with all it's passion, that I loved her, then! I dreamed of returning and claiming her from her parents. Oh! My friend! My father! You can never know the agony I suffered when I found Julie promised irrevocably to another! (*Dropping into chair at table, L. C., his face in his hands.*) She was lost to me, forever!

DOCTOR. Yes, Henri! She was lost to you. Whatever you suffered, you should not have forgotten that Julie is bound in honor and truth to another.

HENRI. To such another. (*Looking up, suddenly, with clenched fist.*) I could have born it as a man should bear the worst, if Julie had been given, in her trusting innocence, to one who might have made her forget that I existed—in the gentle love of a wife and mother. I could have born even that in my own solitude, for I should have known, at least, that she was not unhappy. But a gambler and a profligate! Notorious in every resort of aristocratic vice in Paris! The very money he has gained with her in payment for his title and his family he is spending among men and women as vicious as himself. He will make Julie more and more wretched as years go on. My blood boils like melted iron when I think of it. (*Starting to his feet.*) But I can kill him, now—I can kill him!

DOCTOR. You have arranged for a meeting?

HENRI. Yes!

DOCTOR. If the Count should not meet you?

HENRI. He *will!*

DOCTOR. If he should drop the matter?

HENRI. He cannot!

DOCTOR. I shall try to effect a settlement, Henri. (HENRI *stands and looks at him.*) For the sake of Julie's good name.

HENRI. Her name!

DOCTOR. If you do not hear from the Count before—say, noon, to-morrow—will you promise me to carry out the good resolution which you have so often broken—to leave France, at once?

HENRI. You will tell the Count that I shall wait till noon to-morrow to hear from him?

DOCTOR. Trust me, Henri. I shall be as careful of your honor as you could be yourself.

HENRI. I know you will. I—I give you the promise.

DOCTOR. Try to forget your sorrows in your profession, Henri. Be a hermit, hereafter, in the modern Religion of Science

HENRI. My dear, old friend. (*With a warm grasp of the hand. He moves* R., *pauses at door. Aside.*) The Count *will* meet me!

[*Exit, up* R., *through apartment.*

DOCTOR. If I can prevent this duel, it will be the first time the Count de Crebillon has ever hesitated to meet a man who has once aroused his passion or offended his honor. It is a curious fact in human nature that men who do most to sully their own honor are always the most sensitive when other people trifle with it.

(*A long and piercing, but distant, scream from a woman without, up* L. *The* DOCTOR *starts, listens and goes to door, up* L., *where he looks out. He shrugs his shoulders, turning away.* KATE *runs in from garden, in alarm.*)

KATE. Oh! Doctor! (*Going to him.*) Did you hear that scream?

DOCTOR. Yes. It was startling at first, but I once heard a similar scream in the garden.

KATE. What was it?

DOCTOR. The footman was kissing one of the maids. (KATE *draws back.*) If he'd been murdering her, she couldn't have thrown more agony into her voice. When a woman screams, she screams. The girl didn't seem a bit grateful when I rescued her.

KATE. Captain Gregory has run back to see what it was.

DOCTOR. He was in the garden, with you?

KATE. Yes. (*Looking down.*)

DOCTOR. I didn't hear *you* scream. I hope the Captain won't meet one of the maids. Some of them are very pretty.

KATE. But, Doctor, I can't help feeling there was something more in that cry than you imagine. A few moments ago, as I was picking out the path among the trees, I saw a woman peering into the house.

DOCTOR. Indeed?

KATE. She was not dressed like a servant, so far as I could tell in the shadow of the tree under which she was standing. A ray of moonlight fell across her face. Our eyes met for a second, and she suddenly disappeared. When I heard that scream, just now, Doctor, the picture of that woman's face seemed as clear in my mind as when she was looking into my eyes.

DOCTOR. What was the face like?

KATE. It was pale and thin; a hard, cold face, yet it must have been beautiful once.

DOCTOR. Was the figure of that woman——

KATE. Tall and slender.

[*Enter the* COUNT, *from garden, up* L.]

DOCTOR. Ah! Count! You were in the garden—you heard the voice just now?

COUNT. Yes. I presume it was merely some poor wretch in charge of the police—(*Walking down* L.)—in the street beyond.

KATE. Do you think that was it, Doctor?

DOCTOR. I dare say.

KATE. Poor creature! I pity her. (*Going up; then, suddenly, aside.*) I must get Pierre to run out and post my letter to father, and I'll put in another postscript. I'll ask papa for his consent. I'm quite sure, now, the Captain will propose to me before the next steamer. [*Exit, up* R., *through apartments.*

DOCTOR. Count, you have arranged for a meeting with Henri.

COUNT. Yes; to-night. Will you accompany us, Doctor? I shan't give you much trouble with the boy. I'll only wound him slightly—in the arm or the wrist.

DOCTOR. If you and Henri Saint-Hilaire meet, you will not separate until one of you has received a fatal wound.

COUNT. Indeed! It is a serious passion with him, then? If the young man insists, of course, we must carry it through in his own way. (*Then, with sinister significance.*) Do you think there is any doubt as to *which* of us will be wounded fatally?

DOCTOR. Not the slightest doubt. You are one of the coolest, most experienced and most formidable duellists in France; he is a young student of science, whose only knowledge of the weapons you will use is such as every young Frenchman acquires in the ordinary course of his education. But there is enough blood upon your soul, already, Count.

(*The* COUNT *starts, nervously, looking at the* DOCTOR, *then walking up stage. He turns up* C, *glances out,* L., *quickly and nervously, walks down* L., *touching his forehead with his handkerchief.*)

COUNT. What do you mean?

DOCTOR. Two men have fallen victims to your unerring skill in the duelling field.

COUNT. Oh! (*With relief.*) I am in no humor to-night to talk of these subjects.

DOCTOR. M. Saint-Hilaire will wait to hear from you until noon to-morrow. He has given me his promise that if he does not hear from you by that time he will leave France, at once.

COUNT. Very well. Settle it as you like. I will not challenge him.

(*Exit*, R. 1 E. *The* DOCTOR *looks after him a moment, then walks up* L. *He looks out to garden; glances back at the door*, R. 1 E.)

DOCTOR. "Merely a poor wretch, in charge of the police." The voice did not seem as distant as that, to me. The first Countess de Crebillon committed suicide in the gardens at Monaco, three years ago. She was an adventuress, and a fugitive from justice at that time. I never saw her, myself, but she was tall and slender and said to be very beautiful. (*Looks out a moment in thought, then glances at the door*, R. 1 E.) The night air will be refreshing. [*Exit to garden.*

[*Enter the* DUC, R., *from apartment.*]

DUC. I wonder where Miss Kate is? I've been trying to arrange the matter of our marriage for the last six months. My creditors are getting anxious. I don't understand this American way of conducting matrimonial affairs. Our own way is much simpler. One arranges it all with the girl's parents, and that's the end of it.

[*Enter* KATE, *up* R., *from apartment. She runs across, up stage, looking out*, L.]

KATE. The Captain hasn't returned yet. I begin to think he did meet one of the pretty housemaids. (*Turns down; stops, suddenly, seeing the* DUC, *who is down* R.)

DUC. Miss Kate!

KATE. Duc!

DUC. I received another letter from your father this afternoon. I've been looking for you in the drawing room.

KATE. Sit down.

DUC. Here! Alone?

KATE. Yes! Alone! I wont hurt you. (*Sits*, L. C.) I'm not afraid of being alone with a gentleman, and my father isn't afraid of having me. (*Aside.*) If my reputation can't stand that, I'm perfectly willing to lose it, and the first French woman that finds it is welcome to it. I dare say she'll need it. (*Aloud.*) Sit down.

DUC. Certainly! (*Sitting*, R. C.) Whenever I say anything to you about our marriage, Miss Kate, you refer me to your father; and when I write to him he seems to forget it for about a month each time, and then he refers me back to you. If we were all on the same side of the ocean we could get on faster.

KATE. When you first fell in love with me, Duc, we were three thousand miles apart. I appreciate the compliment very highly. Of course, your interest in me increased very rapidly as the steamer on which I left New York approached the coast of Europe, at the rate of eighteen miles an hour.

DUC. I—I don't quite follow you, Miss Kate.

KATE. Concerning my dowry——

DUC. Ah—yes!

KATE. Now, you do follow me. What do you think your title, including yourself, is worth, cash! Will two million francs do? Father will pay you that amount.

DUC. Two million francs! (*Rising.*)

KATE. On the day you and I are married.

DUC. My solicitor will draw up the contract at once.

KATE. Oh! No! (*Rising.*) We cannot possibly sign the contract yet, Duc. Being an American lady, I must insist on following the customs of my own country. Before a marriage contract can be duly ratified, in America, there must be certain preliminary formalities, which propriety there demands. The gentleman is expected to make love to the lady, and to win her heart.

DUC. I'm sure I shall be delighted to pay the most devoted attention to you, Miss Kate. I will make love to you with pleasure. (*Approaching her and attempting to press her hand. She withdraws it.*)

KATE. Not personally, Duc! You misunderstand me. A lady and gentleman, in America, always make love to each other through their lawyers!

DUC. Their—lawyers? Oh!

KATE. If you will kindly send me the name and address of your solicitor, I will also engage one, and they will enter into negotiations on the subject; when I am duly advised by my own lawyer that you have won my heart, I will sign the marriage contract, but not till then, Duc. (*Walks up.*)

DUC. (*Aside, down R.*) What a very remarkable country! There are so many queer things in America. Half the gentlemen in the smoking-room had something extraordinary to tell about America, and they all said Miss Kate told them so.

KATE. (*Looking out. Aside.*) The Captain is coming up the path. (*Aloud.*) I don't think it is best for us to be alone, together, any longer, Duc.

DUC. No. I will retire. (*Rising; then aside, going.*) I wonder how long it takes a lawyer to win a lady's heart? [*Exit, R.*

KATE. Captain Gregory won't need a solicitor! (*Looking out; then turns down stage.*) He was just going to ask me to be his wife, as we leaned over the curb of the old well, together—his eyes were looking straight up into mine, from the water—when I ran away from him. The word "yes" was so close to my lips, if I hadn't run away, I'd have answered him before he'd asked me the question. And I had just let him catch me again, under the old oak with mistletoe on it, when we were interrupted. I'll let him finish the question, now. Ha, ha, ha! A woman in love is like a girl playing kiss-in-the-ring; she runs away until she's afraid she won't be caught; then she stops. (*Dropping on otto-man.*, R. C.) I've stopped.

(*Folding her hands, demurely, as if waiting. Enter the CAPTAIN, up L., from garden. He looks at KATE, then takes a book from the table, L. C., looks at her again, sits on ottoman, L. C., opens the book. She looks at him.*)

I hope he hasn't stopped playing kiss-in-the-ring. (*Aloud.*) What book are you looking at, Captain?

CAPTAIN. (*Reading title.*) "The Code of Social Etiquette in France, by Mme. la Countesse de Bassonbille."

KATE. Aunt gave that to me to study. She thought I needed it—badly.

CAPTAIN. Some one has been marking it. (*Reads.*) "If you desire to wed a young girl"——

KATE. Oh! That is such a curious passage. I marked that double, you see.

CAPTAIN. Oh! It was you!

KATE. Eh! (*Then dropping her head.*) Yes, I did it. (*Aside.*) All the parts marked are about how people get married.

CAPTAIN. (*Aside.*) I never yet took up a girl's book that everything like that wasn't marked in it. Perhaps this will tell a fellow how the French fellows manage it, when they're in love. It may help me. (*Glances at her, then reads aloud.*) "If you desire to wed a young girl—(*Glances at her again.*)—you must get a mutual friend to make the first advance, or you may get the clergyman, or the family lawyer."

KATE. Ha, ha, ha, ha!

CAPTAIN. An officer in Her Majesty's service might as well ask the clergyman or a family lawyer to charge a battery for him. But the French way isn't so bad, after all. Miss Kate—(*Rising.*) —I—I wish I had some one—a lawyer or a clergyman, or some-thing—(*Approaching her.*)—to—to say—exactly what I want to say to you. I'm only a soldier, you know.

KATE. Did you ever read Longfellow's poem, "Miles Stand-ish?" The hero and heroine were alone, together, as you and I are, and she said to him—the hero's name is John——

CAPTAIN. The same as mine——

KATE. So it is.

CAPTAIN. What did she say to him?

KATE. "Why don't you speak for yourself, John!"

CAPTAIN. Eh? Speak for myself?

KATE. That's what the girl in the poem said.

CAPTAIN. Oh! What did that John answer?

KATE. Oh! Well—he ran away without saying a word.

CAPTAIN. Oh! Did he? (*Walks away, L., thinking.*)

KATE. But, Captain, he came back again——

CAPTAIN. (*Returning to her, quickly.*) And he told her he loved her—I'm sure he did! I love you, Miss Kate, with my whole heart.

(*She starts to her feet, turns towards him with her eyes dropped, then extends both hands, frankly.*)

KATE. And I love you —(*He seizes her hands, eagerly.*)—too earnestly and too sincerely to disguise it. I know that you are brave, and good, and true. I am very, very glad you love me.

CAPTAIN. I tried my best not to love you, because I have nothing to offer you but a—a sword, and a heart, and a pair of spurs, and a uniform, with me in it. But I couldn't help loving you! May I write to your father? This very night?

KATE. I have written to him. (*He stares at her.*) I put in another postscript.

CAPTAIN. Oh!

KATE. I knew you were going to propose to me, six weeks ago.

CAPTAIN. I wish I'd known it as soon as you did. We'd have saved a lot of time. I must join the regiment sooner than I expected. I—I—I wish we could get married before I go. I'm sorry your father is so far away.

KATE. I'll send him a cable. (*Runs to escritoire. Writes.*) "To Robert G. Shipley, Park Avenue, New York. I am going to get married."

CAPTAIN. I hope he'll give his consent.

KATE. Oh! A mere formality like papa's consent can come by mail—(*Still writing.*)—after we are married. I'm only telling him the facts now. (*Writes.*) "I love him very, very, very much" (*Speaks.*) Three "verys"—at forty cents a word; they're worth it!

[*Enter* MME. FONBLANQUE, *up* R. *She stops, up* C. KATE *writes.*]

"Please send me your blessing and enough money for my trousseau."

MME. F. (R.) Alone! With a gentleman!

KATE. There! (*Rising and going to him,* L. C.) If you'll take that to Brown, Drexel & Shipley, the bankers, to-morrow morning, they'll send it for me.

CAPTAIN. I—I would like to give you—just one honest, English kiss.

KATE. You may—and I will kiss you, because I love you, John!

(*They kiss.* MME. FONBLANQUE *gives a short, sharp, bark-like scream, drawing up, stiffly. The lovers start and shrink back a little, left of* C)

MME. F. I am utterly astonished, my niece! I am petrified!

KATE. Captain Gregory has asked me to be his wife.

MME. F. And you have allowed him to kiss you. Worse than that, you have kissed him!

KATE. We love each other.

MME. F. Shocking!

KATE. Why, aunt, dear, a kiss is the only seal that nature has given us for a marriage contract. Kiss me again, Jack!

(*He kisses her.* MME. FONBLANQUE *drops into a chair, with a little scream.*)

CURTAIN.

ACT III.

FIRST TABLEAU.

SCENE.—*The Chateau Fonblanque. Another apartment. Corner of the room, up* C. *Large opening to a hall, up* L. C. *Bay window, up* R. C. *Sunlight on foliage beyond window, with a few rays falling inside. Doors,* R. 1 E. *and* L. 1 E. *Ottoman, up* C. *Arm chair,* R. C. *Ornamental table,* L. C., *with chair.*

DISCOVERED.—JULIE, *standing up* C., *her head resting, wearily, against the casement of the bay window.*

JULIE. The very spots of sunshine on the grass seem like shadows this morning. I am growing blind—blind to everything that used to make life beautiful and bright. Life! What is life, to cling to? What is life, now, that I should fear to lose it? I dreamed, last night, that I was sleeping, and Henri was planting flowers in the earth above me; I was sleeping so quietly and peacefully. (*She reaches up and picks a small branch of leaves falling through the casement from a vine.*) He and I planted this vine together. (*Walking down.*) I used to scold the gardener if he ever touched it. One day, I overheard the old man say that he feared his little mistress would water that vine with her tears some day. I didn't know what he meant then, but I do, now—I know, now! (*In chair,* L. C., *dropping her head onto her arms on the table, and sobbing.*)

[*Enter the* COUNT, R. 1 E. *He stops,* R., *looking at her.*]

COUNT. In tears, madam?

(JULIE *looks up at him, brushes her eyes, quickly, and rises.*)

JULIE. You have returned to the chateau earlier this morning than usual, monsieur.

COUNT. You were weeping because I did not return still sooner. (*Crossing to her.*) You pay me a very high compliment; the more so as I spend so many of my nights away; and I frequently do not return at all the next day. But, now I think of it a second time, it is just possible that your tears have not been flowing for *me*. Pardon me.

(*He takes her wrist in his left hand, quietly, and is about to take the branch of leaves in his other hand. She struggles, very slightly. He presses her wrist, firmly, looking at her; then takes the leaves from her fingers, turning away. She starts, as if to take them again, but restrains herself.*)

It is late for the dew to be lingering on the leaves, and yet there are drops upon these. I fear I was flattering myself; perhaps your tears were falling for another. Pray, do not check them on my account, madam. We, all of us, have sad memories; but we should feel sadder still to lose them. Their roots must be moistened with our tears, now and then. But the autumn is at hand, and every leaf must soon fall—(*Picking the leaves off and dropping them to the floor.*)—one after another. Memories, too, must fall away, one by one, from our lives. (*Turns. R.*) I am sorry that I disturbed your thoughts at such a sacred moment. I came to offer you an apology. I so far forgot myself, last evening, as to interrupt you and M. Henri Saint-Hilaire in one of those emergencies when every considerate husband is expected to be elsewhere. But even the most scrupulous of husbands will make a mistake, now and then, unless he is given fair notice that his presence is undesirable. I trust you will forgive my indiscretion. There was no intentional breach of etiquette, on my part, I assure you.

JULIE. I beg of you, monsieur, to say whatever you have to say to me at once.

COUNT. I will detain you only a moment. At the earnest solicitation of Dr. Girodet, after the incident last evening, I consented to—to give the young man his life.

JULIE. Dr. Girodet sent me word that the matter had been settled—amicably.

COUNT. I claim no merit for my magnanimity, however. M. Saint-Hilaire is to leave France to-day.

JULIE. Yes.

COUNT. And I haven't the slightest objection to have a man passionately devoted to my wife—if he is five thousand miles away. Perhaps it would be unreasonable to object to my wife's devotion to him—even to a former lover—at such a distance. But I have one thing to say to you, madame. I have never dreamed, for a moment, that I was the happy possessor of your affections. And, if I remember correctly, I have never spoken to you of love.

JULIE. Never.

COUNT. Pardon my frankness if I say that I have no interest in that subject. Whatever my faults may be—and I do not profess to be perfect—I am not a hypocrite.

JULIE. You have never deceived me, in that respect.

COUNT. But I *have* an interest, madame—a very serious interest—in my honor as a husband—before the world. That is in your keeping. I shall protect the name I bear—at all hazards. Whatever blots there may be on our family escutcheon, that of cowardice has never been there. Do not forget that you, also, bear my name.　　　　　　　　　　　　　　　　　　　　　[*Exit, up L.*

JULIE. His honor as a husband! His name! I never should have borne it! Father! Mother! You have given me a greater burden than my poor weak nature can bear. Oh, that my dream last night were true. I long to be asleep—asleep. Why should I not be? (*She sees the leaves on the floor, picks them up, quickly and nervously; goes to door.*) Henri leaves me to-day—forever!
　　　　　　　　　　　　　　　　　　　　　　　　　　[*Exit, R. 1 E.*

[*Enter* MADAM FONBLANQUE, *up L., in elegant morning wrapper.*]

MME. F. I have not recovered, yet, from the shock which I received last night. If I had seen Julie, herself, kissing a gentleman, I should have been less bewildered. Julie, at least, is a married woman, and has the privilege of deciding upon her own course in matters of that nature. For an unmarried girl to be guilty of such an action is unpardonable! (*Down* L. C.)

[*Enter* FONBLANQUE. *up* L., *in morning wrapper.*]

FONB. Good morning, Mathilde. (*Kisses her hand.*)

MME. F. Good morning, my husband.

FONB. I trust you have slept well, after the dinner and the reception last evening.

MME. F. I have been somewhat troubled in my sleep.

FONB. I am very sorry. I have passed a restless night, myself. (*Moving* R.) I can't get it out of my head that we forgot to invite some very important personage, in high position, to our reception. It has been quite like a nightmare to me. I feel certain that some calamity has occurred, or is about to do so. And among my letters, this morning, I find a note from the Prefect of Police.

MME. F. What can the Prefect have to say to you?

FONB. He requests me to meet him, in a private room at the Prefecture, at one o'clock to day.

MME. F. What can it mean?

FONB. I have been asking myself the same question ever since I opened the note. It is couched in the most courteous terms possible, of course, to one of my social position. But it is so particularly polite. I was quite startled when I read it. If I had committed a murder, the authorities couldn't have treated me with more respectful consideration. It seems that Dr. Girodet had something to do with the matter; his name is mentioned by the Prefect.

MME. F. Possibly that may explain his very sudden disappearance last evening. I saw nothing of him after about eleven o'clock. But I supposed a professional engagement had called him away.

FONB. You, also, have been troubled in your sleep, Mathilde?

MME. F. About our American niece, Phillippe. I have just sent Pierre to say to her that I wish to see her here. A calamity did occur at the Chateau Fonblanque last night.

FONB. You alarm me!

MME. F. I don't wonder you had a nightmare.

FONB. Relieve my suspense!

MME. F. I saw Kate Shipley kissing Captain Gregory!

FONB. I cannot believe it!

MME. F. With my own eyes!

FONB. A young girl cannot possibly kiss a gentleman—in France.

MME. F. She learned how to do it in another country. What is worse, Phillippe, she told me, to my very face, and in his presence, that she *loved* Captain Gregory.

FONB. Mathilde! (*Dropping into chair*, R. C.)

MME. F. What is still worse, she's going to marry him!

FONB. And discard a duke! I can believe anything of the girl after that. Poor Victorien! Our cousin had set his heart upon her fortune—I would say—upon Kate.

MME. F. I had looked forward to their marriage with so much pleasure.

FONB. I hoped to have given the child my blessing, in the absence of her father. How much is it that the duke owes us, now?

MME. F. Three hundred thousand francs.

[*Enter* KATE, R. 1 E., *dressed for the carriage. She is adjusting one glove, the other in her hand.* MME. FONBLANQUE *sits,* L. C.]

KATE. Aunt, dear, good morning; uncle! I was dressing to go out when Pierre brought me your message, or I should have come down at once. I am going to make a call, in Paris. Julie has kindly lent me her carriage this morning. What did you wish to say to me, aunt?

MME. F. I wish to speak with you, seriously, about the very remarkable incident which came under my personal observation last evening.

KATE. Remarkable, aunt? A gentleman, whom I love very dearly, proposed to me; I accepted him, and afterwards I kissed him. That is the regular order in which we American girls do those things. The next time I see Captain Gregory I shall do it again. Here, I believe, the lady waits until she is married before she kisses the man she loves, or any other gentleman.

FONB. You have so far forgotten your duty to us, your present guardians, as to—to choose a husband for yourself?

KATE. Yes, uncle. I have chosen for myself; and I much prefer to kiss the man I love, before marriage, to kissing one I do not love, afterwards. We are very particular about what is proper in a woman. We do not think that even a marriage ceremony, without love, can make a kiss modest or womanly. I have something serious to say to you, aunt. Do you remember, on the day I first arrived, I said that, if I ever found it impossible to please you, without sacrificing my own self-respect, I should cease to be a visitor at your house? I feel, aunt—and uncle—I am very sorry to say it—but that has come! I have followed the dictates of my own heart; you take a view of what I have done which neither my father nor I can accept; and my self-respect compels me to leave the Chateau Fonblanque.

MME. F. I will not say, then, what I had intended, when I sent for you—that it is no longer desirable for you to remain here.

KATE. Thank you, aunt, for not saying it. I was about to call on the friends from New York, the family I crossed the ocean with; they have returned to Paris. I know they will be glad to have me with them, at their hotel. I will go there, to-morrow, with your permission.

FONB. But what may your father——

KATE. Oh! anything I do will suit papa; it always does. Aunt, dear, forgive me for all the trouble I have been to you. I tried, very hard at first, to act as if I wasn't an American girl, for your sake. But I am, aunt, and I couldn't help being one—if—if all the armies in Europe surrounded me, with their bayonets pointed at the prettiest bonnet I have. Ha, ha, ha, ha! Sometimes I've been a very wicked girl, too; but I couldn't help that, either. That wasn't because I'm an American girl, aunt. It was just because I'm a girl. No girl can help that—I don't care where she was born; only girls in different countries have different ways of being wicked. We American girls have discovered some new ways: that's all.

MME. F. You have acted very wrongly, indeed.

KATE. Our first trouble of all, aunt, was about a dressing-maid.

MME. F. You refused to have one.

KATE. I felt that she would be in the way, especially when I was dressing.

MME. F. She should have accompanied you whenever you walked out, and you would not allow her to do so.

KATE. I found that I didn't care to be responsible for her morals.

MME. F. Julie's governess took charge of you, at my own request, after Julie was married. Madam Rabeau informed me, in less than a week, that *you* had taken charge of *her*.

KATE. I was compelled to, aunt; I saw that she needed careful watching. Besides, I used to give her lessons in the studies you asked her to teach me. But still—as I said before—I *have* been very wicked. I've told more fibs since I've been in Paris than half a dozen girls ought to tell in the same length of time. I don't tell fibs, at all, in New York, now. But, somehow, when one of us American girls comes to Europe—well, if people *will* believe everything one says about things at home, how can any girl that likes fun help telling fibs? Please say to Field-Marshal Corlette, uncle, that he needn't be afraid of going to America for fear of losing all his wigs.

FONB Wigs?

KATE. I'm afraid he got an idea from me that it's dangerous to wear hair at all in the United States. It isn't dangerous, uncle, except when its natural. And I told the Arch-Duke Contagowskoff that I never saw a dinner party with more than one course until I came to Europe. That isn't true, uncle; we often have two courses, and once I was at a dinner where they had three. The Prince de Molzrieaux remarked to me, last night, that he hoped some day to go to America and shoot buffaloes. I told him there were plenty in Central Park. That *is* true. There are two buffaloes in the Park; and they *are* plenty. But the Prince may have received a wrong impression. The Spanish Ambassador is a widower, and he doesn't intend to remain so, I believe; he told me he had heard that American gentlemen had an enormous amount of money. I said I didn't know anything about that, but when a New York girl wanted some pin money, she telegraphed to her father, and he sent it up in a wagon. Later in the evening he asked me for my father's address. Tell him for me, uncle, before he has time to write that I–I was—exaggerating—a little. Papa never sent me anything but a handcart full in all my life. And I told the Marchioness de—the fat Marchioness, aunt—but I haven't time, now, to tell about all the wicked fibs I've told 'em.

FONB. You need not take that trouble. Hereafter whatever information our friends may have received about America——

KATE. Tell them it isn't true, uncle ; and you may say I did it. I'm *very* sorry, indeed, but my health would have broken down if I hadn't done it !

[*Enter* PIERRE, R. 1 E., *a letter in his hand.*]

PIERRE. (*To* KATE.) A note for you, ma'm'selle, from Madame la Countess.

KATE. (*Taking note.*) For me, Pierre ?

PIERRE. Madame asked me to give it to you as she was leaving the chateau, a moment ago. (*Walks up* L.)

MME. F. Did the Countess say where she was going, Pierre ?

PIERRE. She did not, madame.

KATE. She has taken her carriage, of course.

PIERRE. No ma'm'selle. The carriage is still waiting at the door for yourself. [*Exit, up* L.

KATE. A note from Julie, for me. (*Opening it.*) You will pardon me ?

MME. F. and FONB. Certainly.

(KATE *glances at the note, starts slightly, catches her breath, but recovers herself, as if not to arouse their attention.*)

KATE. Julie merely wishes me to make a purchase for her in the Boulevard des Italien.

FONB. (*Rising.*) I will write to your father and tell him how sorry Madame Fonblanque and I both are that your visit has come to a conclusion.

KATE. Thank you, uncle, dear.

FONB. (*Aside.*) I really shall miss the girl very much. I like her.

(*Exit, up* L. MME. FONBLANQUE *crosses*, R. *front, turns.*)

MME. F. We shall both be deeply grieved, my niece.

KATE. I shall be as sorry to leave you, aunt, as you will be to have me leave.

(*Exit* MME. FONBLANQUE, R. 1 E. KATE *returns, suddenly, to the letter in her hand; reads it.*)

"My darling, darling Kate ; I can bear the misery no longer. You are stronger and better than I am, but you—and you only — can understand me. Tell father and mother—oh !—tell them nothing. My room will be empty. That will be enough for them to know. Julie." She has fled—to the man she loves ! The carriage is at the door. I will follow her !

(Turning quickly, to go up. Enter the COUNT, *up* L. KATE *stops, suddenly.)*

Count!

COUNT. Mademoiselle, you are in haste.

KATE. *(Passing him.)* Yes, monsieur, I have an engagement.

(Moving up, as he walks down. She stops, C., *as he crosses,* R., *and sees the miniature in his hand dangling by the ribbon. She speaks, aside.)*

He has Julie's miniature of Henri in his hand.

COUNT. You are looking at this trinket. I just picked it up on the grand staircase. It is a portrait of M. Saint-Hilaire. He may as well take it to South America with him. I will return it to him, in person, with my compliments.

KATE. *(Aside.)* Ah! He will find Julie there.

COUNT. *(Looking at his watch.)* A quarter to twelve; there is only just time.

KATE. Pardon me, Count, but—that is my picture.

COUNT. Yours!

KATE. I have been looking for it everywhere.

COUNT. A gentleman does not give his portrait, framed in gold and set in diamonds, to a mere friend.

KATE. I am very glad you have found it.

COUNT. M. Saint-Hilaire is fortunate. And Captain Gregory? Madame Fonblanque informed me, last evening, that you had chosen him as a husband; I congratulate the Captain, especially on the fact that his rival is going away before your marriage. Husbands are not always so fortunate. Permit me. *(Offering the locket.)*

KATE. *(Taking it.)* Thank you.

COUNT. When M. Saint-Hilaire is gone—you will marry Captain Gregory, of course; but your heart will be unoccupied. If I could hope——

KATE. You addressed me in a tone like that once before, Count!

COUNT. I did; on the occasion of our first meeting—in the train, near Rouen. But we were total strangers, then. We are not strangers, now. On the contrary—I know you perfectly.

KATE. *(Aside.)* Oh! if there was someone near to resent his insolence! *(Aloud.)* You say you know me, Count; know this— I hate you! [*Exit, up* L.

COUNT. Ha, ha, ha, ha! That woman *would* be worth fighting for. I've never quite forgiven the girl for playing the prude with me so successfully, when we first met. She compelled me to apologize to my respected father-in-law, on her account; and she has been laughing in her sleeve at me all the time; carrying on her intrigue under my very eyes. M. Saint-Hilaire is general in his attentions. My own wife is merely one among other ladies in the circle of his fancy. I mistook a boy's passing fancy for the serious passion of a man. Dr. Girodet was wrong. The young Lothario would have been quite contented with a slight wound in his arm. I might arrange a meeting with him, yet. No, I'll keep my word with the Doctor. Besides, it's Captain Gregory's turn now. (*Walking, L., laughing, lightly.*) I'll not interrupt Miss Kate and M. Saint-Hilaire. (*Stops suddenly, with a change of expression.*) Or was the girl lying to me? (*Rings bell, sharply.*) Was it she who dropped that miniature on the grand staircase?

[*Enter* PIERRE, *up* L.]

I wish to speak with the Countess.

PIERRE. Madame la Countess left the chateau a few moments ago, monsieur.

COUNT. Order the carriage at once.

PIERRE. The carriage is out with——

COUNT. The coupé, then! Tell the groom I am in haste.

PIERRE. Yes, monsieur.

(*Exit, up* L. C. *The* COUNT *moves to door,* R. 1 E.)

COUNT. M. Saint-Hilaire leaves France to-day. I will bid him good-bye! [*Exit,* R. 1 E.

CHANGE.

SECOND TABLEAU.

SCENE.—*Apartments in the Rue de Rivoli. Large window at back, showing Paris beyond. Day-time. Doors at* R. C. *and* L. C. *set at an angle of about 45 degrees, half facing the audience. The door at* R. C. *well up stage; that at* L. C. *about 3d entrance. The furniture and ornaments of the room are such as are suitable to a rich, young, French gentleman and scientist who has gathered many objects of curiosity and scientific interest in foreign lands. Table up* C.; *chair near table. A long, low ottoman or lounge,* R. *An ottoman down* L. *Duelling rapiers crossed above window, at back, with wire masks, pads, gloves, etc.*

DISCOVERED.—ANDRE, *on step-ladder at back, getting down the masks, pads, rapiers, etc., from over the window.*

ANDRE. This is the suddenest move my young master has made yet. At one o'clock this morning, M. Henri wakes me up and says: "Andre! Have everything ready to leave Paris this afternoon for South America." It never does take us long to start for a place a few thousand miles off. When we left Brazil, seven months ago, M. Henri said: "Andre! We will start for Paris in two hours." Two hours!—And fifteen boxes of curiosi-

ties and scientific rubbish, besides our portmanteaus! Thank
Heaven! we're going to leave all the scientific rubbish behind
this time. But wherever master is, he'll need his fencing tools,
of course. A pair of rapiers in a gentleman's room serve to defend his honor by implication, so to speak.

(*During the above he has got the various articles from the
wall and descended, placing the ladder near door, and the
masks, gloves, etc., and one of the rapiers on the table, c. He
now stands down c., with one of the rapiers in his hand.*)

His honor! I'm very glad I haven't any honor to defend. Susanne divides her kisses about equally between the barber and
me. All right; she has enough kisses for us both, and some to
spare for the baker. But when a *lady* divides her kisses like that,
two of the gentlemen fight about it, and she kisses the third gentleman while they're doing it. That's honor. Ha!

(*Striking a position, suddenly, L. C., fencing vigorously, with
an imaginary foe, his back to door, R. Enter* HENRI, R.
He stops, looking at ANDRE, *who continues fencing, stepping
back step by step.* HENRY *pats him on the shoulder.*)

Pardon, monsieur! I was imagining myself a gentleman.
  HENRI. Is everything ready?
  ANDRE. Everything; except the rapiers. (*Laying the one in
his hand on the table, across the other.*) You told me to get them
down, but not to pack them up until you gave me further orders.
  HENRI. No! There has been no caller, nor a letter, while
I've been out?
  ANDRE. Your friend, the English officer, was here, monsieur.
  HENRI. Captain Gregory?
  ANDRE. He said M. le Docteur Girodet had told him you were
going to-day, and he asked me what train you would leave by,
as he would like to meet you at the station; but I could not tell
him.
  HENRI. Go to Captain Gregory's apartments, Andre, in the
Rue Scribe, and say that I shall be here until two, at least I
am sorry I was out when he called.
  ANDRE. Yes, monsieur. (*Going; takes ladder over his shoul-
der.*) What orders shall I leave with the janitor?
  HENRI. Tell him to send me any note or letter at once.
  ANDRE. And visitors?
  HENRI. He may let them come up. Hurry back.
  ANDRE. Yes, monsieur. (*Going, R.* HENRI *takes up one of the
rapiers, at the table.*) I'll run around and kiss Susanne good-bye.
The baker is never there at this hour.
                    [*Exit,* R., *with step-ladder.*

  HENRI. Not a word from the Count de Crebillon, yet. Dr.
Girodet has succeeded. I cannot thank him for his good offices.
I might have saved her, or the Count delivered *me*, from a future
that both of us dread to meet. (*Puts down the rapier and looks
at his watch.*) Twelve o'clock. There is no hope, now; and I

can only keep my promise, and my resolution, broken so often, to leave France. (*Dropping upon ottoman, down* L.) How vividly I remember the day I left Paris, two years ago. (*Looks up over his shoulder at the door,* R.) Come in! (*Listens.*) I was mistaken. When I bade her farewell, that day, there seemed to be a look in her eyes which said; "Come back to me, Henri." I dared not say anything of my hopes, then, for fear that they would vanish, as day-dreams do, when we speak of them to others. (*A timid knock at the door,* R. HENRI *rises.*) Come in!

(*Moving forward a step. The door slowly opens and* JULIE *enters.* HENRI *stops,* L. C., *looking at her. She enters, timidly, her hand on the side of the door, her eyes dropped. She moves down* R. C., *her eyes still fixed on the floor, and with faltering steps. She at last glances up at him and moves quickly to the ottoman, falling upon it on her face.*)

JULIE. Don't think that I'm a bad, wicked woman, Henri, but I shall die if you leave me with him. I couldn't help coming to you; I couldn't help it.

HENRI. Julie!

(*He springs forward, crossing to her; leans over her; hesitates a moment, eager to seize her in his arms, but holding himself back by a strong effort of the will; then forces his hands behind him and moves back a few steps.*)

You—you have fled from your home—to me!

JULIE. What will you think of me—what *must* you think of me?

HENRI. I think—that they have driven you to despair.

JULIE. I have chosen between this and death.

HENRI. I am too near despair myself, Julie, to save you.

JULIE. I have taken my choice between a life which I could endure no longer—and your contempt.

HENRI. My—contempt!

JULIE. You can never love me now as you used to.

HENRI. I would not lose, for all the world, Julie, the respect for you which has always been a part of my love. I have worshiped at a shrine, and I would not dare to violate its sanctity now.

JULIE. Oh, Henri! Why have they robbed me of a love like yours? (*Rising.*) I will not rob myself of such a love. I said that I had chosen between your contempt and death. I did not choose rightly.

HENRI. (*Standing.*) What do you mean?

JULIE. Since we parted, last night, my thoughts have wavered a thousand times. When I left home, to-day, I did not know where I was going. It was only from a last, sudden, desperate thought that I came to you. When I knocked at your door, the world became darker than it had ever been before. I seemed to be extinguishing the only light that had been left to me. But you do still love me? (*Turning to him.*)

HENRI. (*Seizing her hand.*) Never so much as I do now.

(*She kisses his hands, passionately, then suddenly tears herself away from him and starts up towards door.*)

What will you do? (*He springs after her and detains her.*)

JULIE. (*Turning and looking at him.*) I will take your love with me, Henri, to another world.

HENRI. Julie!

[*Enter* KATE, *up* R. *She steps in, suddenly. The glove held in her hand in previous scene is now gone.*]

KATE. M. Saint-Hilaire—(JULIE *walks down* L. HENRI *steps* R.)—I came here to save my cousin from herself—and from you, monsieur. (*Moves down to* JULIE). Julie—my darling! (JULIE *turns and buries her face in* KATE's *bosom.*) Come with me, dear! You must return to your home. Whatever you suffer there, you will find more misery still in leaving it. The carriage is at the door. Come, darling!

(*A knock, firm and decided, at the door,* R. KATE *and* JULIE *start.* HENRI *turns, quickly, goes to door and places his hand on the knob*).

HENRI. (*In a low voice.*) In that room for one moment—(*Pointing to door,* L.)—until I can dispose of my visitor.

KATE. Yes. Julie, come!

JULIE. No! (*Drawing up; then, half aside.*) I would sacrifice everything—life itself!—for his love—but—(*Aloud*)—I do not care for the world, now. Let them come in, whoever it may be. (*The knock repeated.*)

KATE. (*Glancing,* R., *then in her ear.*) It may be the Count!

JULIE. I will meet him. (*Then, with a sudden thought.*) But Henri's life! Ah!

(*She hurries out at door,* L. KATE *pulls it shut, secures the knob, carefully; she then turns to* HENRY, *quietly.*)

KATE. There, monsieur. It's all right, now. Your visitor may come in.

HENRI. (*Advancing towards her.*) But you, Miss Kate!

KATE. I?

HENRI. Your own reputation!

KATE. Oh! thank you. I forgot I had one to lose, too. (*Going.*) I'm not accustomed to these French situations.

(*Exit at door,* L. HENRI *moves to door and throws it open. He starts, slightly, and steps back.*)

HENRI. Count de Crebillon! (*Inclining his head.*) Enter, monsieur.

(*Moves down, across to* L. C. *Enter the* COUNT. *He stands a moment at door, looking at* HENRI, *then turns to close it*

(He stoops down and picks up KATE'S *glove from threshold, with-out.)*

A personal call from you is an unexpected honor, Count.

COUNT. I can quite believe that my visit was unexpected, M. Saint-Hilaire. *(Glance at table.)* I see you have weapons at hand; not with any hostile intent, I trust.

HENRI. I did expect to use them. I supposed that I should have seen your own representative before this time.

COUNT. You did not meet Dr. Girodet again, last evening? *(Walking down,* R.*)*

HENRI. He was called away, suddenly, I believe.

COUNT. You must have wondered that you did not hear from me. I assured the Doctor that I would pass over the little incident that led to a misunderstanding between us. I have apologized to the Countess already. Permit me to apologize to you, also.

HENRI. I am not in the humor for jesting with anyone, much less with you, and upon such a subject.

COUNT. *(Looking up, sharply, at him.)* You will find, M. Saint-Hilaire that I can be in earnest, also—in deadly earnest; I have found a lady's glove upon your threshold.

HENRI. Well, monsieur?

COUNT. And the carriage of the Countess de Crebillon is wait-ing upon the street below—at your door! I will drag my wife from your room, monsieur!

HENRI. Pardon me, Count—*(Moving to before door,* L.*)*—but you shall not enter my private apartment.

COUNT. With your permission or without it, I will enter that room.

HENRI. Without it, then, monsieur.

(They face each other a moment, with set teeth. The COUNT *then moves, quietly, up to the table, takes one of the rapiers and moves down* R.*, facing* HENRI. HENRI *steps to the table, takes the other rapier, and moves back to the door, facing the* COUNT.*)*

COUNT. Stand aside, monsieur!

HENRI. You shall not enter!

(The COUNT *lunges forward, fiercely. Two or three quick passes. A scream is heard within the room.)*

COUNT. Aha, monsieur!

(He attacks HENRI *with great vigor and angry determina-tion. A knock at door,* R. *The combat continues. The knock repeated. Enter* CAPTAIN GREGORY.*)*

CAPTAIN. Fencing, gentlemen?

(They stop, suddenly, dropping the points of their weapons.)

COUNT. *(Walking down* L.*)* Monsieur Saint-Hilaire and I are practicing, Captain.

CAPTAIN. Without your masks, or the pads and gloves. It's dangerous sport. Glad I found you in at last, Henri. Thanks for sending round for me. I'm sorry you're going. (HENRI *staggers*.) I say, old fellow!

(*Springing forward and supporting him. HENRI drops the rapier. The CAPTAIN places him in chair near table.*)

You are wounded!

HENRI. A little thrust in the side. Only the point; a mistake. The Count and I—were—so interested—we both forgot ourselves for a moment.

CAPTAIN. (*Feeling HENRY's side and putting his handkerchief to it.*) You Frenchmen find as much amusement in this sort o' thing, I dare say, as we Englishmen do in punching each other's heads.

COUNT. I will get something for your wound, monsieur, and you will need water. I can find it in this room, I suppose? (*Moving to door, L. C.*)

HENRI. Ah! (*Trying to spring up.*)

CAPTAIN. (*Restraining him.*) Hold on, old boy! The wound will be a serious one, if you go on in this way.

COUNT. You must avoid excitement, monsieur.

[*Exit at door, L. C.*

HENRI. Coward!

(*With a quick struggle, releasing himself from the CAPTAIN. He snatches up the rapier and springs toward the door. The CAPTAIN seizes him and forces him by main strength back into the chair, holding him firmly as he proceeds.*)

CAPTAIN. I think I understand the situation; its all in dead earnest, I see. But there shan't be murder on your soul, Henri, so long as I'm a stronger man than you are; and I'm likely to be for some time to come.

(*The CAPTAIN stands with his back to R., as he holds HENRI. The COUNT re-appears, L. C., coming in backwards and bowing.*)

COUNT. Mademoiselle! (*Enter KATE, L. C.*) I ask a thousand pardons!

KATE. Captain Gregory—here!

(*The CAPTAIN turns and sees KATE; falls back a few steps, R.*)

CAPTAIN. Kate!

COUNT. M. Saint-Hilaire! I ask your forgiveness, also, for my intrusion at such a moment. (*Putting rapier on table. Aside.*) The little American devil—(*Walking down R.*)—was telling me the truth after all.

KATE. (*Aside.*) What must he think of *me!* But I must play the part to the end—for Julie's sake.

(*Moving a step forward, L. C. HENRI rises and stands before the door, L. C. The COUNT stands down R., tapping one hand with the glove.*)

COUNT. Ha, ha, ha! A pretty little glove!

KATE. I must have dropped it—after I left the carriage. May I trouble you for it?

COUNT. I am almost tempted to keep it. I envy you, monsieur; or perhaps I ought to envy Captain Gregory. The hand to which this glove belongs has been promised to him in marriage. He will be obliged to share its caresses with other men.

(*An angry start from the* CAPTAIN, *up* R. C., *but he restrains himself.*)

But, all the same, it is a very pretty hand.

KATE. (*Aside.*) I must still endure his insolence.

COUNT. If you can so far overcome your English prejudice against duelling, Captain, as to defend your honor against M. Saint-Hilaire, I shall be very glad to act as your second.

CAPTAIN. The relation which I bear to the lady's hand, Count, is my own affair, not yours.

COUNT. By all means; I would not intrude for the world. One serious word to you, mademoiselle; you will please not borrow the Countess de Crebillon's carriage, with the family crest on its panels, the next time you have a disreputable intrigue with a gentleman. Whatever ideas of propriety may happen to prevail among the ladies of America——

CAPTAIN. (*Stepping forward.*) Permit me to return Miss Shipley her glove, Count.

COUNT. Certainly, Captain!

(*Handing him the glove, with a bow. The* CAPTAIN *draws back his arm and strikes him violently in the face with it.*)

CAPTAIN. I have succeeded in overcoming my English prejudice against duelling, monsieur.

COUNT. I am quite at your service, at any time, after you have met M. Saint-Hilaire. He has a prior claim upon your honor. Of course, I cannot meet you, as a gentleman, until you have settled that claim.

CAPTAIN. M. Saint-Hilaire is wounded.

COUNT. Ah! I forgot! Whenever you please, Captain.

CAPTAIN. I have orders by telegraph to be in London to-morrow morning.

COUNT. Very well; at once.

CAPTAIN. Thank you. (*He turns to* KATE, *with the glove.*)

KATE. Not—not for me—you must not fight—for me!

CAPTAIN. May I take this with me?

KATE. (*Eagerly.*) You still value it?

CAPTAIN. May I take it?

KATE. Yes. (*The* CAPTAIN *turns up* R.) But you must not risk your life for me!

CAPTAIN. We have no time to lose, Count.

(*Exit, up* R. C. *The* COUNT *follows him up; turns at door.*)

COUNT. I go with one of your lovers, mademoiselle, and I leave you alone with the other. I am sorry that I am not a third.

KATE. Ah! (*With a burst of anger.*) I have had enough insults from you, Count, and from your race. (*Moving towards him.*) I have a protector, now. With all my heart, I hope he will *kill* you!

COUNT. We shall see!

(*Exit. R. KATE staggers with sudden weakness, supporting herself by chair, R. C.*)

KATE. What will be the end! (*Then, with a sudden thought.*) Henri!

(HENRI *springs toward her from door, L. C., placing the rapier on table and putting up his arms to support her.*)

Not me—not me—I can take care of myself. Julie! She fainted when she heard your swords: I left her on the balcony.

(HENRI *starts towards door, L. C. He stops, bringing one hand to his breast and wavers, on his feet. KATE continues, not seeing him, and looking away, R.*)

He still loves me; but, if he fall, his last thought of me will be—what? John!

(HENRI *falls backwards, towards the audience, at full length. She turns.*)

Henri! Henri!

(*She falls to her knees at his side, her hand on his heart.*)

CURTAIN.

ACT IV.

SCENE.—*The Chateau Fonblanque. Same scene as that of Act I. The double doors open, showing drawing-room at back, and the furniture re arranged. The large table up R. with small chair at the left. Arm-chair at right of table. Arm-chair up L., near mantel. The other pieces of Act I. to taste.*

[*Enter the* DUC DE FOUCHÉ-FONBLANQUE, *through drawing-room, his hat in his hand.*]

DUC Phillippe is out! Extraordinary circumstance! He has taken his nap at this hour, regularly, for the last twenty years. I wonder if he, also, is one of the parties to the duel. His name wasn't mentioned at the Club, though nearly everybody else's was.

[*Enter* MME. FONBLANQUE, R. 1 E., *in elegant wrapper.*]

Ah! Mathilde!

MME. F. Victorien!

DUC. Sorry to disturb you at this hour; Pierre said you were dressing for the evening; but—do you know anything about the affair this afternoon?

MME. F. What "affair?"

DUC. Ah! You havn't heard of it at all, yet? There are all sorts of rumors at the Club. Somebody has been fighting a duel with somebody else.

MME. F. Indeed!

DUC. Whether anybody killed anybody or not, nobody can find out, but everybody says somebody was killed. The police arrived on the spot just in time to see the carriages drive off, in accordance with their regular instructions. I called at the Count's private apartments, in the city, on the way here, but all I could get out of the janitor was, the physician had left instructions that he wasn't to be disturbed.

MME. F. The Count was concerned in it?

DUC. A gentleman at the Club was looking out of the window, and he saw Dr. Girodet going rapidly by in a carriage, and the Count lay back on the seat with his face very pale.

MME. F. Really, Duc, I trust that nothing serious has happened to my dear son-in-law, the Count. You have aroused my curiosity.

DUC. So it has mine. Captain Gregory's name has also been mentioned in connection with the affair, but that is evidently an error. A member of the Club told me that one of the other members had been told by another gentleman that he had just seen the Captain walking, quietly, on the Boulevard. He asked him to join him in a drive to the Bois, but he thanked him, kindly, and said he wished to finish his cigar. M. Saint-Hilaire was one of the principals in the duel.

MME. F. Henri! (*Very earnestly.*)

Duc. Dr. Poncilett was called to attend him. One always gets the latest news at the Club, but it sometimes requires deep thought to understand it. It's very difficult to put this and that together. The Count was wounded with a broad-sword. M. Saint-Hilaire was shot. They were fighting each other. I have it all on the highest possible authority.

Mme. F. I hope Henri's life is not in danger !

Duc. Let me offer you my sympathy. I have heard that Henri's father and you were deeply in love with each other, before you were married.

Mme. F. Considerations of family made our union impossible. But—H–s–h—(*Looking around.*)—M. Fonblanque knows nothing of the circumstance.

Duc. Trust me implicitly, Mathilde. The same individual can hardly expect to monopolize a woman's hand and her fortunes, and also her affections. I'm sure my cousin Phillippe is too well-bred to be so unreasonable.

[*Enter* FONBLANQUE, *up* R.]

Fonb. Ah, Cousin Victorien!

Duc. Phillippe, have you heard anything about——

Fonb. It has come to you already, then ?

Duc. I was just telling Mathilde——

Fonb. I dare say every one at the Club is talking about it. The simple truth is this ; it is a mere ordinary case of suicide.

Duc and Mme. F. Suicide !

Mme. F. Henri Saint-Hilaire !

Duc. The Count !

Fonb. They have nothing to do with the matter. The Prefect of Police——

Duc. I understood the police didn't interfere.

Fonb. On the contrary, they have the entire matter in charge, and they have managed it with the utmost discretion.

Duc. The duel !

Fonb. I received a notice from the Prefect this morning.

Mme. F. Oh, yes ; what was it, Phillippe?

Duc. It occurred this afternoon.

Fonb. It occurred last night.

Duc. I—I wonder if we are talking about the same thing.

Fonb. The Prefect was extremely polite to me, and he assured me he was conducting the investigation as a mere matter of routine formality. There are half-a-dozen similar cases in Paris every day. In the present instance, the woman——

Duc. Ah ! We hadn't got to the woman, in the Club, yet, but we were all looking for her.

Fonb. A total stranger took the liberty of committing suicide in the gardens of the Chateau Fonblanque last evening.

Mme. F. In our own grounds?

Fonb. The fact was discovered by Dr. Girodet, about half-past ten. He communicated with the police at once. The Prefect is a personal friend of his, and he was considerate enough to conduct the affair without disturbing us or our guests, Mathilde. It was extremely kind on his part. It would have been very embarrassing, indeed. It annoys me exceedingly as it is.

MME. F. Do they know who it was?

FONB. There was nothing whatever to identify the person, and the Prefect trusts that I shall hear nothing more of the unfortunate incident. I am sorry it has got to the Club, cousin.

DUC. It hasn't. I was speaking of another matter entirely.

MME. F. Victorien was saying that our son-in-law, the Count——

FONB. Oh! by-the-bye, I rode to the Bois after I left the Prefect. The Marquis de Polignac leaned over from his carriage and remarked that he hoped the news he had just heard was not true—that the Count de Crebillon had been seriously wounded in a duel. You can imagine my feelings as a father. After a turn or two more in the Bois, I told the coachman to drive home, at once.

DUC. I believe the Count is seriously wounded.

FONB. I wish you would learn something definite about it. I'll go and take my afternoon nap; it is two hours after my usual time. If anything of special interest transpires, Mathilde, you may have the servant wake me.   [*Exit, yawning*, R. 1 E.

MME. F. M. Fonblanque and I are both very anxious about the Count.

DUC. I'll drive down to the Club again.

MME. F. Do, Victorien. I'll finish my dressing, now. (*Going.*) Au revoir, cousin.

DUC. Au revoir. [*Exit*, MME. FONBLANQUE, R. 1 E.] I feel anxious about the Count, too. I bought a little mare from him yesterday morning, and yesterday evening he offered to lay me three to one against her the first time I raced her. I'd like to get a few points about her. I hope he isn't seriously wounded. It's very queer, but I never do buy a horse from a man that he doesn't offer me the odds against it.

(*Going up* L. *Enter* KATE, *through drawing-room*, L. *She moves in rapidly, coming down* R. C., *without seeing the* DUC, *who stops, up* L. C.)

KATE. The servants here have heard nothing. Five hours of agony and suspense since he left me to meet the most dangerous duellist in Paris! I could not stay longer with Julie. Perhaps uncle or aunt have—— (*Going*, R.)

DUC. Miss Kate.

KATE. Oh! Can you tell me, Duc? Has any news come of——

DUC. The duel?

KATE. Yes! Captain Gregory!

DUC. The Captain is severely——

KATE. Wounded!

DUC. No! I've got everything mixed up this afternoon; everybody says at the Club that somebody——

KATE. O—h!

DUC. I was going back to learn something more definite.

KATE. Yes—go—by all means—at once !

Duc. I'll return presently, with the exact facts. [*Exit, up* l.

KATE. What torture ! I can learn nothing. The Captain has not returned to his apartments. I felt like a mad woman in the street, and everything going on as if his life were not at stake. I have nowhere to turn. (*Dropping into the chair up* l.)

[*Enter* CAPTAIN GREGORY, *with* PIERRE, *in drawing-room.*]

CAPTAIN. On second thoughts, Pierre——

KATE. Ah !

CAPTAIN. I'll not disturb M. Fonblanque—(*Walking down* R. c)—if he is taking his afternoon nap.

KATE. Alive !—and safe !

CAPTAIN. I will leave a note. I merely dropped in to pay my respects before leaving for London to-night, and to see Miss Shipley.

KATE. To see me !

CAPTAIN. Has she returned to the chateau ?

PIERRE. Ma'm'selle is here, monsieur.

CAPTAIN. Oh ! I beg your pardon.

KATE. Captain—Gregory !

CAPTAIN. Will you excuse me one moment, Miss Shipley ? I wish to leave a note with Pierre for M. Fonblanque.

KATE. Oh—certainly ! (*He sits at table*, R. c.) A note ! and I am absolutely dying to know what's happened.

CAPTAIN. (*Writing.*) "My dear M. Fonblanque : Being compelled to return to London this evening, I dropped in to say good-bye to Madame Fonblanque and yourself, and to apologize for shooting your son in-law. With warm regards to you both, I remain——" It's lucky for me I do remain. The Count is a good shot.

KATE. (*Aside.*) I'm choking ! (*Aloud.*) Captain !

CAPTAIN. One moment. (*Addresses it.*) Pierre, you may give this to M. Fonblanque, with my card—(*Rising.*)—but don't disturb him. [*Exit* PIERRE, *up* R., *with note.*] Yes ?

KATE. And you are unhurt, thank Heaven ! But I hope you have not killed him.

CAPTAIN. I really can't say.

KATE. He—fell ?

CAPTAIN. Yes.

KATE. He may be dying—now !

CAPTAIN. Possibly. But I'm under the impression he isn't.

KATE. You fought with swords !

CAPTAIN. No.

KATE. Pistols !

CAPTAIN. Yes.

KATE. You met in the field, your seconds gave the word, you fired !

CAPTAIN. Yes.

KATE. The Count was wounded—go on !

CAPTAIN. That's all.

KATE. Oh! you Englishman! you'd let a woman die gasping for knowledge. Do tell me something about it!

CAPTAIN. You've told me.

KATE. You have heard nothing since?

CAPTAIN. No.

KATE. Oh! John! To think that you may have killed a man.

CAPTAIN. I'm sorry to say that I may have killed a number of men, while I was fighting for my country, when I didn't see half as much good to be gained by it, though the members of the British Cabinet did.

KATE. Captain Gregory, you have risked your life, to-day, to defend me from an insult, because I was a woman; but you found me in a—in a most compromising position. I cannot explain to you why I was there; but I need not say—that—you are—free—from your obligations to me.

CAPTAIN. Oh!

KATE. Of course—our—our engagement is at an end.

CAPTAIN. Ah!

KATE. After what has happened, there can be—no further relations—between us, of any kind.

CAPTAIN. M—m.

KATE. (*Aside.*) He might show some interest in the subject, even if he does despise me.

CAPTAIN. You were in the private apartment of another gentleman.

KATE. Yes, I was; and that ought to excite some kind of emotion in *any* girl's lover, even if he *is* an Englishman!

CAPTAIN. You were there—with the Countess de Crebillon.

KATE. You know the truth?

CAPTAIN. I know it now.

KATE. How?

CAPTAIN. You've just told me.

KATE. Oh!

CAPTAIN. I *guessed* it was the Countess. I've been long enough in France for that, and I thought you wanted the Count out of the way at that particular moment. But I knew one thing absolutely—whoever it was, *you* were not there alone.

KATE. Why did you know that? (*Advancing.*)

CAPTAIN. (*Approaching her, looking full into her eyes and speaking very earnestly.*) Because my confidence in you is as strong as my love!

KATE. Ah! (*Clasping her hands, joyously.*) You fought the Count because you believed in me?

CAPTAIN. I'm too good an Englishman to risk my life for a woman that isn't worth fighting for!

KATE. Jack! (*Resting her head on his breast.*)

CAPTAIN. You remarked just now that our engagement was at an end.

KATE. Never! 'till I'm your wife!

(*Fondling him, with his head between her hands, looking into his face. She suddenly gives a little cry and leads him down by the left ear, which is tipped with black court plaster.*)

You are wounded!

CAPTAIN. I forgot to mention that. The Count's bullet took the tip of my ear off.

KATE. You were so near to death as that? My own pet British Lion!

(*Embracing him, then resting her head on his shoulder. He takes the glove from a pocket.*)

CAPTAIN. I've brought this back to you. (*Holding it up.*)

KATE. You may keep it now, John.

CAPTAIN. Until the hand that fits it is mine!

KATE. My knight!

CAPTAIN. When I looked at that on the way to the field, I felt, somehow, that the Count was in danger.

KATE. The Count! (*Drawing back.*) Oh, Jack! Jack! I hope you haven't killed him.

CAPTAIN. I hope so, too.

[*Enter the* DOCTOR, *in drawing-room,* L.]

KATE. Dr. Girodet! (*The* CAPTAIN *glances up and walks,* L., *to mantel.*) Now we shall know the worst. I dare not ask him! (*Walking up* L C.)

[*Enter* FONBLANQUE, *up* R.]

FONB. Ah! Captain, you are still here. The servant has just given me your note and card.

CAPTAIN. I asked him not to disturb you.

[*Enter* MME. FONBLANQUE, R. 1 E., *now in afternoon dress.*]

MME. F. Captain!

CAPTAIN. Madame!

FONB. Mathilde, I have just discovered that we omitted to send an invitation, for last evening, to the Austrian Ambassador.

MME. F. Is it possible! (*Very anxiously.*) How very, very unfortunate!

FONB. It has quite broken up my afternoon nap. I couldn't sleep at all. It was you, by the bye, Captain, who had a duel with our son-in-law this afternoon. (*Sitting,* R. C.)

MME. F. The Captain! (*Pleasantly.*) Then you can tell us something about it. (*Sitting,* R.) Do you happen to know the result?

CAPTAIN. The Count has been under Dr. Girodet's care. (*The* DOCTOR *advances,* C.)

FONB. Francois, I trust you can relieve the very painful tension which suspense has produced in the minds of Madame Fonblanque and myself.

DOCTOR. When we left you on the field, Captain, we drove as rapidly as possible to the Count's apartments in Paris. After reaching there, he fell into a restless slumber. When he awoke, I was standing at his bedside. I told him that he had only a few minutes to live.

KATE. Oh! (*Sinking into the chair up L. C.*)

DOCTOR. The Count turned pale, and he trembled like a frightened girl. The frequently-tested courage of the duellist failed him at that moment. Gamblers are always superstitious, and men who are most ready to risk their lives in the field of honor shrink with absolute horror when the Angel of Death hovers over them in the stillness and loneliness of the sick-room. These facts in human nature quite agree with a theory of mine in the study of psychological phenomena in their relations to the functions of physical life. I once had a prolonged discussion with Professor——

KATE. But—Doctor!

DOCTOR. Pardon me. This is a digression, and you, of course, cannot share the interest in the subject which I feel as a scientific man. The Count came more and more under the influence of some secret terror that convulsed his frame. At last he told me to open a small drawer in a cabinet. I did so, and I found a picture there, of a woman. He whispered in my ear that I would find a face like that in the deserted well of the Chateau Fonblanque. I answered him that I had already seen it there. While our friends were entering the chateau, last evening, by the carved mahogany doors, the body of a dead woman, an unbidden guest, passed silently out through the little gate in the garden wall. The first Countess de Crebillon had confronted her husband.

MME. F. The first Countess!

DOCTOR. She might have confronted a tiger, in the jungles of India, with less danger. The Count has never allowed trifles to stand in the way of his own good fortune. Your daughter, cousin, has never been the Countess de Crebillon.

MME. F. Julie!

FONB. My daughter!

DOCTOR. The Count did not know until that moment that his wife was still living. They were separated when the official mistake at Monaco occurred, three years ago. It had become her interest to disappear from the world, and she took advantage of the mistake, until her husband's second marriage and his renewed wealth made it to her interest to return to life.

KATE. Oh! John! John! (*Sobbing, in her chair.*)

DOCTOR. What is it, my dear?

KATE. The Count! A human being's death is upon my—my husband's soul.

DOCTOR. Not at all! The Count will be perfectly well in a week!

(KATE, MME. FONBLANQUE *and* M. FONBLANQUE *start to their feet, the* CAPTAIN *starts around, all looking at the* DOCTOR.)

KATE. You said he had only a few moments to live!

DOCTOR. I told *him* so; and I am under great obligations to you, Captain, for giving me an opportunity to act as an amateur detective. Your bullet went just near enough a vital part for my purpose. But it was quite harmless, I assure you. It is in my waistcoat pocket at the present moment. The Count's written confession is in another pocket.

KATE. My Jack! (*Moving down to* CAPTAIN, R.) You haven't killed a man, after all.

DOCTOR. From a scientific point of view, the experiment was an interesting one. It illustrates this fact : The unusual activity of the nerve centers in the brain, popularly known as "conscience," can be excited artificially. In other words, there is no actual physical necessity for men to wait till they are dying before repenting of their sins. I shall prepare a report of the case for the Academy of Science. How is your ear, Captain?

CAPTAIN. Very well, I thank you—what there is left of it.

FONB. Mathilde, my dear, we must speak to Julie.

MME. F. She left the chateau this morning, Phillippe, and she has not returned yet.

KATE. Julie is at the bedside of the man she loves, uncle; and she can remain there, innocently, now. M. Saint-Hilaire has been very severely wounded.

FONB. Henri is wounded, too?

MME. F. Henri!

FONB. I—I trust he will recover.

KATE. The physician says that he may, with careful nursing; and Julie will give him that.

DOCTOR. Let us hope that he will recover, cousin. Let us hope that you have not robbed a brave young lad of his life, and your own daughter of her happiness, for the sake of the Fonblanque family. (*Returns up* R. C.)

MME. F. (*Aside.*) He was your son, Isidore!

FONB. (*Aside.*) Pauline, you were Henri's mother! (*They turn, slowly, catch each other's eyes, and draw up. Both sit.*)

[*Enter the* DUC, *up* L., *quickly.*]

DUC. We've got all the facts at the Club, now. Captain Gregory is dead!

(*General attention. The* DUC *sees the* CAPTAIN, *puts up his glasses, and stares at him.*)

I had it on the highest possible authority!

KATE. It isn't his ghost, Duc. (*Turning to the* CAPTAIN *and putting her hand in his.*)

CAPTAIN. If it is—(*Dropping his arm about her waist.*)—It isn't so bad being a ghost.

DUC. I beg your pardon, Miss Kate—but——

KATE. Oh! Ha, ha, ha, ha! I forgot all about the—the business affair—between us, Duc. Captain Gregory has been his own solicitor.

DUC. I really don't understand you.

DOCTOR. I hope your creditors will wait, Duc, until a Frenchman *can* understand an American girl.

KATE. I will write to papa. He will find a place for you, if *I* ask him, in one of the railway companies he owns.

DUC. A place—for a duke—in a railway company!

KATE. I dare say you can marry in New York. A few of our girls, a very few, but still a few, are quite willing to pay the debts of European noblemen.

DUC. Telegraph your father, please; perhaps he knows a girl like that. (*Turns up* L. C.)

[*Enter* PIERRE, *up* L.]

PIERRE. A telegram—for Miss Shipley.

KATE. Oh! (*Taking it. Exit*, PIERRE.) A cable dispatch, from papa—(*Opening it.*)—in answer to the one you sent for me last night. (*Reading.*) " From Robert J. Shipley. Fifty-five words. Get married at once, and bring him to New York." Certainly; of course!

CAPTAIN. Oh! very well; settle it between you.

KATE. " Who is—he?" O-h! Ha, ha, ha, ha! I forgot to tell him your name. But papa has perfect confidence in my judgment. I've given my attention to matters of this kind. Papa hasn't. (*Reads.*) " Would run over to wedding, but there is a corner in Pennsylvania Central."

CAPTAIN. What's a corner?

KATE. I'll explain all those things to you after we're married. (*Reads.*) " Have cabled twenty thousand dollars to bankers in Paris." For my trousseau! (*Reads.*) " And placed two hundred thousand dollars government bonds to your credit here." My wedding present! Dear papa! That's a part of the corner.

DUC. Corners are nice.

KATE. Some folks think so, and some don't. I can't make out this word. (*Reads.*) " B—l." (*The* CAPTAIN *crosses to her*, C.) Oh, yes; my father's blessing!

CAPTAIN. (*Looking over her shoulder.*) So it is! (*Reads.*) " Blessing. Prepaid."

DOCTOR. Very liberally prepaid.

DUC. I hope some New York father will bless me.

CAPTAIN. You shall be my blessing!

KATE. I hope so, Jack! My mother has given me her blessing, too, for I—I am sure it was she that chose you for—my husband.

CURTAIN.

.